THE STORMGLASS PROTOCOL

TIM PRATT
ANDY DEEMER

The characters and events in this book are fictitious.
Any similarity to real persons, living or dead, is
coincidental and not intended by the author.

ISBN 978-0-9899336-0-5

First edition: September 2013

www.stormglass.com

PROLOGUE: FIELD TEST

"Why have you brought me here?" the Doctor asked. He wore a perfect gray suit, standing beside a rolling field of green grass, with one shiny black shoe propped up on the bottom rail of a wooden fence.

The scene would have been one of perfect country beauty, if not for the stinking carcasses of two dozen cows that littered the field, their bodies hideously bloated and misshapen, flies already beginning to gather around their fresh corpses. The stench was almost unbearable.

The assistant swept out his hand. "I thought you should see the results of our fourth test." Other research assistants moved among the dead cows, dressed in white biohazard suits. "The bees are still far too deadly. You can't possibly use them to replace—"

"Ah, ah, ah." The Doctor smiled, raising his massive eyebrows as if remembering a joke he'd heard some days before. "Mouth shut, please."

The assistant removed his glasses and cleaned them on the hem of his sweat-stained shirt.

"But what about the deaths?"

"Why are you so upset? They're only cows."

"This is the fourth time, sir. The flock of sheep in Vermont was horrible, but it's the cats that worry me. The ones near San Francisco."

The Doctor shook his head, and chuckled. "Don't worry. I had my own reasons for choosing that location, and judging from the report I received this morning, my plans are moving ahead nicely. A Stormglass team has already been dispatched."

The assistant frowned. "Stormglass? What does Stormglass have to do with this?"

The Doctor studied his assistant with his ice-cold eyes. "Just tend to my bugs."

"Yes sir," the assistant said, then hesitated. "There is one other problem, though. The rancher..."

"Mmm. He came to check on his cows and found this mess, did he?"

The assistant nodded, trying to suppress a shudder. "Mundt has the man in his van," he said. Mundt was a young man who'd lost one of his arms in a horrible accident, an arm later replaced with a cutting-edge artificial one. When he'd shaken hands with the assistant, he'd squeezed hard enough to bring tears to the assistant's eyes.

"How very inconvenient," the Doctor mused. "We can't have witnesses."

The assistant frowned. "He's just a small businessman, and we've wiped out his entire farm by accident. You can probably buy his silence—"

"There is only one way to absolutely ensure silence, young man, and it's far cheaper than writing someone a check. You know this, and you've known it for seven years." The Doctor gazed up at the clouds again for a moment. "Have you met the twins?"

The assistant closed his eyes, and when he first tried to speak, his throat was suddenly too dry. He coughed. "Only once. They toured the lab." The damage had taken weeks to repair.

"Well, I'm sending them to San Francisco later today, but they have a bit of free time. Perhaps they could see to the rancher."

"Really, Doctor, there's no reason for an innocent man to—"

"Everyone dies, eventually," the Doctor said sharply. "Innocent and guilty both. The only way to win the game is to make sure your enemies die first."

THE SPIES ON GLEAM STREET

Jake's parents were the ones who tipped him off about the spies on Gleam Street, though they didn't mean to.

Jake was practicing stealth and concealment at the time, crouched down in the pantry and coincidentally eating some of his mom's secret stash of VindiqoQo chocolates. He heard his parents come into the kitchen, chatting, and decided it was a good opportunity to hone his eavesdropping skills.

Jake's dad said, "You know that abandoned house over on Gleam Street? The blue one that looks like the roof is about to fall in? I think some squatters are living there. I saw a light upstairs when I was driving past last night, just a flash, for a second."

"Maybe somebody was just checking the place out, looking to buy," his mom said. "I bet it's cheap."

"Maybe. But the front steps are still barricaded with all that trash, so I doubt it. It's a shame. That whole block is falling apart."

Jake took another bite of VindiqoQo and decided to investigate. If someone was using the house for a secret hideout, he wanted to know. You never knew where you might find spies. Or bank robbers on the run. Or a band of ninja assassins.

Summer was pretty boring so far, so he really hoped he'd find something.

After waiting for his mom to go to work, Jake escaped the pantry undetected and told his dad he was going out for a while. He walked a few blocks west and then strolled along Gleam Street, casually, as if on his way to somewhere more pleasant. The library was a block further west, so he had a valid excuse for passing by, and carried a book in one hand just in case.

The house in question was a two-story place with flaking blue paint. The grass in the yard was knee-high, and the windows downstairs were boarded up. It didn't look like anyone was living there, legally or otherwise. But when he studied it closer — pretending to tie his shoes — he could tell things were slightly off. The wooden gate didn't have a padlock, but a dirty outline of one remained. The rusty garage door wasn't entirely closed, either. An inch of empty space at the bottom showed where someone had forced it open and then been unable to shut it completely.

Those small signs of disturbance were enough to take Jake from curious to flat-out interested, so he completed his fake trip to the library, spent a few minutes browsing through the small section of books on magic — he'd read them all, nothing new — and then returned the way he'd come for a second look at the house.

This time he noticed the mess of old buckets, cinderblocks, and rusty paint cans blocking the front door had been moved, the dust and dirt around them disturbed. Like someone had gone in that way, then put the junk back without getting it exactly right. The padlock was back on the gate — and that gave Jake's stomach a little jolt. It meant someone had been at the house that day, just minutes ago, while Jake was at the library!

He pretended to get a leg cramp and hopped one-legged to sit down in the blue house's driveway, where he looked things over while he massaged his calf. From this close up he could see the padlock wasn't locked, just hanging there in the closed position, so it looked secure from a distance.

Somebody was definitely living in the house.

Jake figured it was probably just a homeless guy, but what if it wasn't?

He decided to put the house under surveillance. He didn't have much else to keep him busy that summer. His best friends were off visiting relatives, or on vacation, or at camp, and the neighborhood was a lot less fun without them around, so he'd taken up spying. At least then he wasn't *alone* alone — he was just under deep cover, a solitary agent far behind enemy lines.

Jake stood up from the driveway on Gleam Street and walked back home, already planning his next move. He got into his house and back out again without his dad — who was working away at the computer as always — even noticing his entry or exit. Ten minutes later, Jake sat straddling a branch fifteen feet up a tree, armed with his dad's bird-watching binoculars. He'd never understood the appeal of bird watching. But criminal-watching? That made sense to him.

This particular tree was an old oak, with strong branches and a thick covering of leaves. Jake was pretty sure he was invisible, except when the wind stirred the leaves around, but the people inside the house wouldn't be on the lookout for a spy. The tree stood right across from the blue house, which had been vacant for so long the "For Sale" sign had fallen over and never been put back up again. No wonder the criminals, or whoever they were, chose to hide out here. There was hardly anyone around to see them.

He let the binoculars dangle on his chest by the strap around his neck and wiped his forehead. It was hot today, even in the shade of the tree. Jake had a little water bottle tucked in one pocket of his cargo shorts, and he took that out one-handed, using his other hand to keep a grip on a branch. Falling out of the tree wouldn't be very spy-like. After he took a drink, he lifted his binoculars and looked at the upstairs window again —

And saw someone looking back at him, through binoculars of their own.

SURREPTITIOUS ENTRY

The person in the window had much cooler binoculars than Jake did: black and oversized, with lots of different circular lenses arrayed on little movable arms, like a machine you'd see at the eye doctor. They lowered the binoculars, and Jake saw it was a girl — and a kid — with curly black hair and a long nose and a pointy chin and a scowl on her face.

She vanished from the window, and Jake immediately started scrambling down the tree. *Had she seen him? What if his cover was blown?*

He dropped to the ground and started running toward the end of the block, racing for home. He ran for two blocks before finally looking back, and didn't see any sign of pursuit. Which, now that he was calm enough to think about it, made sense. Even if the girl had seen him in the tree, she was probably more afraid of him than he was of her. Who was she? She hadn't looked familiar, so she probably wasn't from the neighborhood. Was she a runaway?

As Jake walked into his driveway, though, his imagination started to work. What if she wasn't just a runaway? Those incredible binoculars didn't seem like something a runaway would have. But what else could she be? A girl detective? A really young terrorist? Or even exactly what Jake was pretending to be — a secret agent?

At the end of his driveway, Jake paused to look in the mailbox. He didn't understand why they still had a mailbox, since almost nothing ever came — but he still enjoyed checking it, and felt a little thrill whenever there was something in the box addressed to him.

This time, though, he didn't feel the thrill. All that sat in the mailbox was another of those letters.

A heavy off-white envelope, with "Highly Confidential — To Be Read Only By Addressee" penned in red on the front. Jake sighed. He'd gotten three or four of these, and they were always full of stuff about how he was special, and had been chosen for a program, and how he could make the world a better place. But his dad had taught him all about scams and spam, and he figured these letters fit into one of those categories.

After he stepped inside the house, he tore the new envelope open, read the first couple of lines — "Your failure to respond leads us to believe your mail is being intercepted, so we will pursue other avenues" — and then tossed it into the recycling bin.

The distant sound of a computer keyboard clattering away told him his dad was working in the office. Jake cut a slice off the loaf of bread they'd half-eaten at dinner the night before, then drizzled some honey on it. He leaned in the doorway of his dad's office and took a bite, chewed, and swallowed while looking at his father's back.

"I think there are spies living in one of the empty houses on Gleam Street," Jake said. "Or maybe terrorists, I'm not sure. I was up in a tree for a while, doing recon, trying to monitor their activities. One of them looked out a window, right at the place where I was hiding, but I don't think I blew my cover."

"Huh." His dad's voice was vague and far away. He leaned forward to peer at something on his monitor. "When I was a kid we just played cowboys and Indians. Times sure have changed."

"You're not supposed to call them Indians, Dad. They're Native Americans. Indians are from India."

"Right you are," his dad said, but in that not-even-half-listening tone he got sometimes, so Jake rolled his eyes and headed to his room upstairs.

He spent the rest of the afternoon practicing card tricks, but he was still better with the coin tricks. He took out the half-dollar he'd gotten for Christmas, and walked it back and forth across his knuckles. *Not bad*, he thought. He only dropped it when his mind wandered back to that girl with the binoculars. Had she seen him? And who was she? Should he try to make contact with her tomorrow?

"I'm home," his mom called from downstairs, "and I've got pizza!"

They ate together in front of the TV, watching a documentary about a North Korean terrorist called Kim Kyok-un. Jake yawned as the presenter showed where Kim had planted explosives at the Olympics.

"Pay attention, Jake," his dad said. "This is a bad guy."

"But this stuff doesn't affect us," Jake said. "It's not like he's going to bomb us."

"Well, he tried to bomb the Olympics. That's not so far away from here! They say he's been experimenting with EMPs recently."

"What's an EMP?" asked Jake.

"An electromagnetic pulse. It's a burst of energy that shuts down all the electronics in the area. Computers, phones, traffic lights, cars, everything. It would shut down the whole city if he did that, and would allow him to do anything he wanted—"

"Why are we watching this," Jake's mom interrupted. "It's just depressing."

So they switched the channel and watched an old black-and-white film noir thing, which wasn't nearly as depressing as the news.

Later, as Jake climbed into bed, he thought about the girl he'd seen. Maybe he could walk over to the empty house and climb the gate, see what was going on in the back yard. That probably wouldn't count as trespassing, not technically — since I'm just a kid — he thought as he drifted off to sleep.

Some hours later his eyes snapped open, though he wasn't sure why. There must have been a noise, but if so, he didn't hear it again. Jake pushed himself up on his elbows to look around his shadowy room, and had the weirdest feeling he wasn't alone.

"Hello?" he said, tentatively, but no one answered, of course.

Jake threw the covers back, but before he could get out of bed to look around, the standing lamp in the far corner of his room lit up, revealing the dark-haired girl he'd seen upstairs in the empty house, sitting in his chair by an open window. She wore clothes in shades of black and gray, and had strange goggles over her eyes that made her look like some kind of bug.

"Hi, new kid," she said with a sinister smile. "We need to talk."

Jake opened his mouth to yell for his mom and dad, but froze when something cold and circular pressed against the side of his neck. Jake's mattress creaked and shifted as someone sat down beside him, though Jake didn't dare turn his head to look.

A boy's voice whispered close to his ear: "Don't even think about screaming, new kid. Very bad things will happen if you scream."

THE NEW KID

The girl in the chair snorted.

"Very bad things will happen? You're so dramatic, Filby." She turned back to Jake and added, "Although in a way he's right, new kid. Very bad things would happen to us if you screamed, because we'd have to jump out your window, and Filby would probably break his legs when he landed." She looked up again. "Would you please stop poking him in the neck with that flashlight? You're probably scaring him to death."

"The technique worked," the boy — Filby? — argued, "He didn't scream." The cold circle withdrew from Jake's neck, and he turned his head. The boy on his bed was dressed just like the girl, all in discreet black and gray, but he wasn't tall and skinny like her. He was short and chubby, with red hair and freckles, and his goggles were pushed up on his forehead. Filby smiled sheepishly and held up a small metal flashlight, which he slipped into one of the jacket's many pockets. He must have pressed the flashlight into Jake's neck, making Jake think he had a gun. "Sorry about that," he said, blushing a little. "It was all I could think to do. I didn't want to put my hand over your mouth. I got bitten that way once."

"I bit him," the girl said. "That was just before we became friends."

"Who are you?" Jake said. "And what are you doing in my room?"

"We're secret agents," the girl said. "Which you'd know if you actually read your mail. How many letters have you thrown out? Four? Five? So they decided to send something harder for you to ignore. Like us."

"We're here to recruit you," Filby added excitedly. "But then you spied on us. We didn't expect that." He shook his head. "I guess we should have. She said you're promising. How did you find our safe house?"

"The padlock wasn't even closed," Jake said, still confused. "The garage was open. The junk on the porch was moved around. But who are you?"

Filby slumped his shoulders. "We were sloppier than I thought." Then a light bulb clicked. "Or maybe you're just better at this than I thought. Yeah, that must be it! You're exceptionally good!"

The girl coughed quietly to call attention to herself. "Because you showed such promise, new kid, we've been authorized to bring you in on our next mission. Which is good — we could use an extra pair of eyes."

"Extra pair of eyes?" Jake asked, shaking his head. "Is this a game? A joke? Who are you?"

Filby nodded toward the girl. "Her codename is Lizzie Lew."

"Call me Lizzie," she said.

"And I assume you've already figured out my codename. It's Filby. And this isn't a game — you were recruited."

"Recruited? How?" Jake scrunched up his face as he tried to work out if he'd forgotten something important.

"Someone said you'd be a good agent. Someone else investigated you. Someone else approved you. And since you don't read your mail, here we are."

Lizzie jumped in. "So what happens next, new kid—"

"Stop calling me that," Jake snapped. "My name is—"

"Ah ah ah." Lizzie waved her finger back and forth. "We know who you are, but you need to stop using your real name, pronto. We didn't tell you our real names, did we? Your codename is, uh... wait, it's on the tip of my tongue..."

Filby interrupted, "Come on, Lizzie, he's Hale!"

"Yes, that's it — Hale!"

"So the way you offer jobs is you break into people's houses?"

"We actually call it 'surreptitious entry,'" Filby said, turning red.

"And I'm the best at surreptitious entry," Lizzie said proudly, shoving her goggles up to her forehead and revealing her dark, watchful eyes. "Only when it's for a good cause, of course."

"Look, we're members of a secret organization that's protecting the world," Filby said. "And we want you to join us!"

"We're not asking you to say yes right now, new kid – I mean, Hale. We're just here to introduce ourselves. That way, you won't freak out when we show up in the morning."

"Here? Why are you going to do that?"

"We're on a mission," Filby said. "Lizzie and I aren't from around here, so we need someone to show us around. Our cover story is that we just moved into town, and we're brother and sister—"

"Step-sister, obviously," Lizzie said, grinning. "You think anyone would buy us as blood relatives?"

Jake's head was still fuzzy from sleep, and the surge of adrenaline was beginning to fade. These kids were probably crazy, or messing with him... but what if they were telling the truth?

"But who are you really?"

"We can't tell you that," Filby said. "But everything you're feeling, all that doubt and suspicion? That's where we were when we were first recruited. Of course we actually read our mail and followed the instructions, so we were eased into things. Tomorrow you'll see we're telling the truth."

"It just doesn't make any sense," Jake protested. "How can kids be secret agents?"

"We're perfect because we're kids," said Lizzie with a thrilled smile. "Nobody expects us to be secret agents! And if we get caught, adults just think we're kids up to no good. They tell us to get lost, not knowing we're really spies!"

"Not so loud," said Filby. "You'll wake his parents. And don't worry, Hale, we're working for the good guys."

"Just try to keep up with us tomorrow," Lizzie said with a grin. Then she turned and dove headfirst out the open window, which was almost enough to make Jake want to scream.

"She's such a show-off," Filby said, shaking his head. He started toward the window.

"Wait." Jake clutched at the other boy's wrist. "This mission you're talking about tomorrow — what is it?"

"Hopefully nothing," Filby said, chewing his lower lip. "It's kind of strange, though. Something's been happening in different places around the world, dead animals found cold and swollen and, well, yesterday it happened here. Our Echelon Leader wants us to check it out."

Echelon Leader? Jake thought, frowning. *Are these kids for real?*

Filby crossed the room and climbed out the window, much more carefully than Lizzie had — though Jake wasn't sure what he was climbing onto, unless they'd put a ladder against the house. Jake got out of bed and went to the window, but there was no sign of either kid, or a ladder, or anything out of the ordinary at all. The moonlit lawn was completely empty. He closed his window and hooked the latch, then went back to bed. He couldn't sleep a wink. His mind was spinning.

THE FIRST MISSION

Jake yawned through breakfast and didn't eat much, even though his dad made buttermilk-cheddar-bacon biscuits. His mom was long gone by the time they sat down to eat, off to drive through rush hour fueled by nothing but coffee and a VindiqoQo.

"Some kids might come over today," Jake said.

"I thought Aaron and Pete were at camp this week?" His dad swiped at the screen of the tablet computer resting beside his plate, catching up on news or tweets or whatever.

"They are. These are new kids, I just met them yesterday. Filby and Lizzie."

"Mmmm. Well, I look forward to meeting them. Just don't run too wild in the house, I've got a ton of work I need to concentrate on today."

"I think we'll go out." Jake fiddled with his butter knife. "They're secret agents. Investigating some kind of mystery or something. They need my help."

"That sounds fun," his dad said around a mouthful of biscuit.

Jake sighed.

Jake was waiting on his front porch when they arrived. He'd half-expected them to rappel down from his roof or parachute onto the lawn or land in a black helicopter, but they just rolled up to his house on bikes. Very fancy bikes — hers was red, his was blue, but otherwise they were identically sleek, tricked out with mirrors and black canvas saddlebags, with real headlights mounted underneath the handlebars.

"Is that a camera," Jake asked, reaching out to touch a device on the front of Lizzie's bike.

"No touchey," she said, pushing his hand away. "This thing can be dangerous."

"You have a bike, right?" Filby said.

"Not compared to yours." Jake wheeled his old three-speed out of the garage.

Filby looked over the bike, then nodded with a knowing smile. "Don't worry, when you're on assignment, you get better equipment."

"These bikes are pretty sweet," Lizzie said. "See these switches?" She flipped up a concealed panel on one of the handlebar grips, revealing a row of pulsating buttons. "Evasion countermeasures. This one releases spikes from the saddlebags."

"You know they're called caltrops, Lizzie, right?"

"Yeah, whatever. They're little spikes, good for popping tires. This one releases grease, which makes the road turn into a slip and slide. And this one..." She grinned.

"There's an electric motor concealed under the seat," Filby said. "You move fast. Surprisingly fast. It doesn't last long, but it's pretty scary."

"These are nothing, though" Lizzie said. "Wait until you see the welbikes."

"Welbikes?"

Filby rolled his eyes at her. "I don't think Hale's going to be jumping out of airplanes anytime soon."

"Well, you never know in this business. Mount up, new kid. We're on the job."

They set off pedaling, zipping through the neighborhoods, and Jake brought up the rear, wondering whether he should just veer off on his own. Were those buttons on their handlebars really connected to anything, or were these kids just messing with him? The glowing effect on them was pretty cool either way. And the thing was: he was bored. Even if Lizzie and Filby were crazy, crazy could be interesting.

After biking for a while they cruised off the quiet mid-morning streets and veered into Angleton Park, the acres of green that sprawl through the city. Jake's family came here for kite-flying and stuff sometimes, and on sunny weekend days it was full of people strolling and picnicking and throwing tennis balls for their dogs. Today wasn't sunny, and it wasn't the weekend, so the park was almost empty.

"Okay, here's where you come in," Filby said. "We don't have precise coordinates, but we're supposed to go to the big whale." He snorted. "Isn't 'big whale' tautological? Like saying 'little shrimp' or 'wet water'? I mean, the whole point of whales is that they're big."

"There are two whales, though," Jake said. "There's a big one and a little one."

"Ha," Lizzie said.

"Come on, I'll show you."

Jake pedaled through the park, following asphalt trails that gradually dipped downhill, toward the creek bed. There were concrete statues scattered along the creek, pitted by weather and worn smooth by thousands of children climbing over them. Jake wasn't sure if they were art, but among them was a turtle the size of a kitchen table, a dragon's head as big as a couch, and the two whales. One was as big as a cow, with a sculpted waterspout emerging from its head. This of course was the small whale. The other was more the size of a grey truck with an upraised tail.

"Here we are," Jake said as he leaned his bike against a tree.

Filby and Lizzie got off their bikes. Lizzie clambered up on top of the big whale's back and peered around in all directions, as if keeping a lookout. Filby paced around the whale slowly, squinting at the ground.

"Is there a lot of wildlife here, Hale?" he asked.

It took Jake a moment to remember 'Hale' was his code name. "Wildlife? Like squirrels and birds? Sure, there's also a bunch of homeless cats."

"Not any more," Filby said grimly. "A dozen feral house cats were found here, disfigured, swollen and dead."

"Poisoned, I bet," Lizzie said as she hopped down from the whale, landing like a cat might. "But why, how, by who?"

Jake frowned, looking around. "There aren't any dead cats here now, so who's going to tell you that?"

Filby scanned the landscape. "Sometimes you get missions you understand, Hale, and sometimes you don't." He squatted down on one knee, and studied the ground.

Lizzie stood watching him, and then yawned exaggeratedly. "While you look for clues, Agent Filby, I'm going to practice at the range." She wandered down to the creek, and grabbed a handful of pebbles. Jake watched as she fired them across the water, hitting the same piece of floating trash each time.

"She's a good agent," Filby said as he looked up at her, "but she doesn't have the patience for forensic work." He carefully took a smartphone from his pocket — but it wasn't a phone — and tapped on its screen, then waved it slowly along the dirt.

"So what are we looking for?" Jake said.

"Anything out of the ordinary," Filby answered without paying attention.

"Hypodermic needles," Lizzie shouted from the creek. "Matchbooks from night clubs in Monaco. Weird foreign cigarette butts. Whatever."

"We'll gather evidence, and then we'll analyze," added Filby.

Jake shrugged and wandered slowly to the other side of the whale, watching carefully as he walked. He tended to notice things, spotting anything that was out-of-the-ordinary, and had always been great at Easter egg hunts. But would that cause some secret organization to notice him? It didn't seem so likely.

Not that he was seeing much now. There were a couple of coins — just dirty pennies — some goldfish crackers that hadn't been found by birds or squirrels, an empty can of Splurge Soda, a bent paperclip, a dead bug — except it wasn't an ordinary dead bug.

"Hey guys," Jake shouted, "There's a dead bee over here. But it's the weirdest-looking bee I've ever seen."

"Where?" Filby rushed over to his side, leaned forward and stared at the bug without touching it. Jake had seen plenty of bees, of course, and like those this was yellow with black stripes, but it was bright yellow, as yellow as freshly-painted lines down the middle of a street. It was almost as wide as a penny, with long wings and antennae and a curved stinger that was actually big enough to see without even squinting. Jake had been stung once, but that bee's barb had been way smaller than this one. Really, this looked more like a busy bee logo from a cereal box or a jar of honey.

Except dead, so not really very busy at all.

"This could be important," Filby said, and nodded to Jake with a smile.

"Noticing things," Lizzie said, ambling over slowly, "That's a useful skill for a spy. Let me see." She leaned over. "Weird."

"Let's take a closer look," Filby said. He took another device from his pocket, examined it to make sure it was the right one, and held it out. "Here you are, Hale. This is your HyperOpticon. All new agents get one on their first day."

Jake took the device, a small plastic rectangle with pulsating buttons, and realized the plastic was actually a screen, and the buttons read things like 'Zoom,' 'Enhance,' and 'Record.'

Filby turned the bee over with a small pair of white plastic tongs, moving its body gently. "Get some footage of this," he said, and Jake tapped record and pointed the small device while Filby tilted the tongs to show the bee from various angles.

"Okay," Filby said. "Now try zooming in."

Jake obliged, tapping the appropriate button a few times, and the bee swelled in the lens, magnified so far he could see the individual hairs on its body. "What's that on its belly?" he asked.

"Let me see," Lizzie said, suddenly crowding in from behind and leaning over Jake's shoulder. She whistled. "Recognize that, Filby?"

"It looks like some kind of logo," Jake said. Almost hidden in the tiny hairs on the bee's belly, there was a stylized, sharp-edged V.

"Vindiqo," Filby whispered under his breath.

"Like VindiqoQo's? The candy company?"

"They don't just make candy," Filby said. "They're a huge company."

"With ties to criminal gangs," Lizzie added, as Filby glared at her. "What? That's not secret!"

A couple of older kids walked by then, shoving each other and laughing uproariously at nothing in particular. Jake glanced up when they went by — they were twins, dressed in khakis and polo shirts, with short blond crew cuts and bright blue eyes. They looked about fifteen or sixteen years old. One of them kicked Jake's bike as they passed, causing the other one to laugh even louder.

"Jerks," Filby said.

The boys stopped and turned at the same time.

"What did you say, fat boy?" one of them yelled.

TOP SECRETS

"He called you fat," Lizzie said, springing to her feet.

"I'm not fat," Filby said, lifting his mass beside her. "I'm big boned. And it's all muscle anyway."

"Maybe not all muscle," Lizzie said, looking him up and down with a smirk.

"You want a bath, kid?" one of the twins shouted at Lizzie. "Looks like you're ready for a dip in the creek."

Lizzie smiled calmly, and leaned back against the whale. "You could try. I'd like to see what happened next."

Jake looked at his new friends, amazed. Those jerk twins were bigger and older and scarier and... and Lizzie and Filby didn't even seem intimidated.

"Come on," one of the boys said to the other. "We've got better things to do, anyway. Leave the babies playing in the dirt."

"You boys have fun," Lizzie called with a wave as they toddled away. One of them gave Jake's fallen bike another kick on the way past.

But as soon as they were out of sight, Lizzie dropped her smile and turned serious. "Did they look familiar?" she whispered.

"Sure. They look like a million other bullies," Filby said.

"Maybe," she said, her head cocked to one side. "They just seem... do you know them, Jake?"

He shook his head. "I've never seen them before. But weren't you guys worried?"

Filby smiled. "Wait until you get some training, Hale. Practice with Iron Tiger for a few months, and you won't be afraid of jerks like that anymore."

"Iron Tiger?"

"She's a Stormguard coach. Self defense training." Filby lifted his arms into what looked like a confident karate position. "If they tried to attack us, they'd just end up hurting themselves. But they're gone."

"I'm going to look something up," Lizzie said, walking to her bike and opening up the saddlebag, as Filby turned back to the bee.

Jake peered through the HyperOpticon. "Is it some kind of toy bee?" The insect looked awfully real. "Does that company make toys?"

"Sure," Filby said, with a grim laugh. "Tons. Maybe you heard about those baby toys that were contaminated with lead, now banned in most countries around the world — those were made by Vindiqo." He scratched his ear. "Presumably that one was an accident."

"Filby has faith in humanity," Lizzie said, returning with a tablet computer in her hand. It looked like an iPad, but smaller and sleeker and more metal. "Titanium shell," Lizzie said when she noticed Jake looking. "Practically indestructible. I don't like computers, but I love things that can't be broken."

"Like the stinger on this bee," said Filby. Jake reached out, and Filby clamped his hand down on Jake's wrist with surprising strength. "Really, Hale. Don't touch it. I think there's a good chance this is what killed those feral cats."

"Yeah," Lizzie said. "And you don't want to end up like them." She was frowning at her tablet, swiping her finger over the screen occasionally.

"We don't have any pictures of the dead animals," Filby said, "but the parks custodian said they were swollen and deformed, like little balloons were implanted under the skin, covered in tiny red puncture wounds… which make sense if this bee was involved. Lizzie, this is just like what happened in Vladivostok."

"They're definitely connected," nodded Lizzie distractedly.

"But this bee didn't sting anything," Jake said, remembering something from biology class. "Bees are... they're like suicide bombers, right? When they attack, they die. Their stingers are covered in hooks. They get one chance to sting, bam, but they can't pull their stingers out again, and when they try to fly away, they tear themselves apart. This bee still has its stinger."

"Sure, so maybe a cat fell on it and squished it to death," Lizzie said, looking up from her tablet.

"But shouldn't there be lots of other dead bees, with their stingers missing?" Jake asked.

Lizzie groaned. "Thanks a lot, new kid. Now we're going to have to crawl over every inch of this park looking for dead bugs."

"I'll set up a search grid around the incident site!" Filby sounded as excited about setting up a grid as Jake could get about learning a new card trick. He picked up the bee with his tongs and carefully placed it in a small clear vial, like a test tube, only this one boasted a small screen with a digital readout. He then slid the vial into a small metal case, and stowed it in the saddlebag on his bike. "Nothing stronger than tungsten carbide," he said to himself, before adding, "Well, except for 5Cr-Mo-V. But why would anyone use that to protect a test tube? Get your HyperOpticon, Lizzie! This will go a lot faster with three of us searching."

"Hold on, I'm just — huh. Guys, come look at this." She beckoned, and they joined her, looking down at the screen of her tablet. There was a photo, sort of blurry, like it had been taken with a cheap camera phone. It showed two boys, blond, maybe fifteen or sixteen years old, standing in some kind of warehouse, holding hockey sticks. "Do they look familiar to you?"

"What a terrible picture," Filby said. "I can tell they're human, but—"

"They look sort of like those guys who kicked my bike," Jake said. "But it's really hard to tell."

"That's what I thought, too." Lizzie's voice was grim.

"They're not the only teenagers in the world with blond buzz cuts," Filby said, "but there's clearly a resemblance. Who are these guys?"

"Their names aren't on file," Lizzie said. "I don't think anyone knows. This picture was taken by an undercover agent at a Vindiqo warehouse." She glanced at Jake, then at Filby.

"So those kids work for Vindiqo?" Jake asked.

"Stormglass recruits kids, so what would stop Vindiqo from doing it?" asked Filby.

"It would be kind of cool to get to break rules all the time," added Lizzie. "You have to admit, Filby, this does look like them."

He nodded. "Absolutely. Hale and I will search for more bees. You watch out for those twins, and if they come back, get some pictures. I'll run a facial recognition scan."

"You know how to do facial recognition scans?" Jake asked, impressed.

"Wait until you see some of the stuff we can do," Lizzie said as she climbed to the top of the whale to keep lookout again.

Facial scans? Criminal gangs? Jake couldn't tell if the idea was more exciting or scary — but Filby and Lizzie were mostly just treating the possibility like bad news that had to be coped with, so he tried to do the same.

After forty minutes of crawling on their hands and knees, turning over leaves and combing through grass and peering into the creek bed, Filby finally declared the search complete: there were no more bees in the vicinity.

"Someone must have cleaned them up," Filby said. "But at least we have one sample. That should be able to tell us a lot once we get it analyzed."

"So what happens now?" Jake said.

"We deliver the bee to a dead drop, and we await further instructions," Filby said.

"Okay, gotcha," Jake said. He paused. "Just one question, what's a dead drop?"

"Spy stuff," Lizzie said with a smirk.

"Come on," urged Jake.

"It's a way to pass information in secret," Filby said. "There's a place in town, a bunch of them in every big city, where we can leave anything we need to send to headquarters. Another agent checks the location every day, picks up whatever there is, and leaves a reply. We never even see the other agents."

"What kind of places?"

"All kinds of places," said Lizzie. "Behind a loose brick in a wall. Shoved in an obscure book in a library. Inside a fake rock in a park."

"Can't you just mail it?"

"Mail gets stolen," said Lizzie. "All the time."

"Huh," Jake said. "But... can't you just send an e-mail or something?"

"E-mail can be intercepted way too easily," Filby said.

"Yeah, but you can encrypt the messages," Jake said. "My dad says there are codes so impossible to break that even government's computers can't crack them."

"Vindiqo has better computers than the government," Filby said sadly.

"Hey," Lizzie said. "You guys are forgetting the biggest part. How are we supposed to e-mail a dead bee?" She jumped down from the whale. "There's no sign of that pair of idiots, anyway. They're probably nothing to worry about. We'd better head for the dead drop."

"You guys have fun." Jake stood up and stretched his legs. "I think I'm going home."

"What are you talking about," Filby said slowly, as if talking to an idiot. "You can't go home in the middle of a mission."

"You guys are in the middle of a mission. I'm not." He picked up his bike as he continued, "You say you work for some top secret organization, but you haven't told me who, or what, or anything. I know about Vindiqo — they make good chocolate bars — but I don't know anything about who you work for! I'm not going to run all over town with you when you won't tell me anything." Lizzie and Filby paused as Jake climbed on the bike, adjusted the seat, and lifted his arm to wave goodbye.

Lizzie turned to Filby with raised eyebrows, and he shot her a short nod before turning and marching away. Lizzie sauntered over to Jake, put her arm around his shoulders, and walked him off the bike and toward the creek.

"Here's the thing, Hale. Filby knows the rules: you don't divulge operational intelligence in the field. You don't tell people who you're working for. You stick to your cover story. Now, in a perfect world we wouldn't be filling you in. You'd already know everything. In a perfect world where you actually read your mail."

"Hey, I read it! I just didn't—"

"Come on — let me finish. Filby follows the rules, but I don't. So I'm going to tell you some of the things your Echelon Leader should have. I'm only leading you away from Filby so he doesn't have to hear me do it. It makes him twitchy — it's just how he's built."

Jake looked behind him. Filby was prodding at his HyperOpticon, brow furrowed in concentration, the tip of his tongue protruding from one corner of his mouth. Jake looked back at Lizzie.

"He didn't tell you any of that. You guys just, like, looked at each other."

"We've worked together before, and we have an understanding. When Filby looks at me a certain way, it means, 'This isn't in the rule book, so you deal with it,' and when I look at him a certain way, it means, 'This is boring and I will mess it up just to make things more entertaining, so if you want it done right, maybe you should do it.'"

She took a seat on the head of the small whale and looked at Jake's face for a long moment. "So. Let me tell you about who we work for." She took a deep breath and said, "We're from Stormglass."

Jake didn't register any of the surprise, or shock, or excitement that she seemed to expect. He just raised his eyebrows.

"Like Stormglass, the game?"

"It's not a game," she said testily as she pulled back her sleeve. Jake's eyes widened as he saw the jagged knife scar that ran down the length of her arm. "Trust me, it's real. It's an underground force of secret agents."

Jake studied her. She wasn't joking.

"The game is just a front. Stormglass was launched by the United Nations to fight criminal gangs worldwide, but secretly."

"Why is it a secret? If you're fighting criminals, it's good!"

Lizzie nodded. "We are good but lots of the criminals are in the government or run big companies. They have important connections. So the investigations have to be top secret. Stormglass teaches us to be spies, and then gives us little jobs to do. Little things, like trying to save the world."

Jake tried to process it all.

"But if Vindiqo are trying to wreck the world, why would they put their logo on the bee," Jake said, frowning. "It's like they want people to know the bee comes from them"

"What do you think?"

Jake shook his head. "I don't know what to think. It's not a prank, I guess — I don't see how you could fake something like that bee, not without spending a ton of money. And if the bee is real..." He thought carefully before he said the next thing, remembering that long scar running along her arm. But he was sure. "If it's real, I want to investigate it, too. I want to be a Stormglass agent."

"Good." She grinned, and spoke quickly. "Since Vindiqo probably knows who you are by now. Which is why I'd better tell you a couple of other things. First, we use a hand signal to identify ourselves." She surreptitiously hooked the fingers of both hands together to make a pair of interlocking curves, like the letter *S*. "And second... if an adult ever claims to be a Stormglass agent, they're lying, and probably working for Vindiqo. Stormglass adults never contact us outside headquarters. And third, even if another kid introduces himself to you as a Stormglass agent, be suspicious."

"Because Vindiqo recruits kids too, right?" he said. "Like maybe those blond kids?"

"You got it."

"Okay, but... why would anybody go to work for Vindiqo?"

Lizzie snorted. "Like I said, breaking rules can be awesome! More fun than following them, for sure. And don't you know any kids at school who'd jump at the chance to join a group of rich international businessmen and criminals?"

Jake blinked. "Huh. Right. When you put it that way..."

She shrugged. "Being rich would be pretty cool."

THE DEAD DROP

"Okay, he's in," Lizzie called.

Filby looked up from his HyperOpticon. "Welcome aboard, Hale. Let's get to the dead drop. Somebody should be along for a pick-up this afternoon. I've got a map, Hale, but do you know where, let's see, Jabberwocky Books and Comics is?"

Jake nodded. "Sure, I go there sometimes, it's just a couple of miles. I'd better call my dad and tell him I won't be home for lunch."

"I don't have to remind you how important secrecy is to our—" Filby began, but Jake just shook his head.

"I could tell my dad everything I've done today, and he'd just say what an active imagination I have. Don't worry about it." Jake called home, and when no one picked up, he just sent a text instead — his dad paid a lot more attention to those than he did to incoming calls anyway. A moment later, Jake got a text back saying, "ok, call if need anything."

Jake put away his phone and led his fellow agents — *fellow agents!* — through the park toward downtown. The city had spent a lot of money improving the main street, putting in new trees and a nice fountain and better sidewalks, and performing whatever kind of magic cities did to make more stores come along to open their doors. Jabberwocky Books and Comics had been on the street for a long time, though, and still had a kind of grungy dustiness that Jake liked — it looked more real, somehow, than the shiny perfect retail stores on either side.

Jake stopped his bike across the street from the comic shop and started to lock it to a rack. "Don't worry about locking it," Lizzie said, putting her hand on his arm. "I'll stay with the bikes while you guys hit the drop. It'll only take a minute anyway." She grinned. "That reminds me, though. One time Filby convinced the tech lab to make a bike—"

"Come on," Filby interrupted. "Don't tell that story."

"No, it's great! So Filby somehow convinces the tech lab to make him a bike with this special lock, where you just press your fingerprint to a special pad and it locks the wheels in place. So nobody can ride off with your bike, right? Well-" Lizzie was starting to laugh as she spoke. "The first time Filby left the bike on a sidewalk without chaining it up, somebody picked it up and just carried it away!" She was doubled over, laughing so hard she could barely speak. "I bet they never broke the lock, though!"

"It was a good idea." Filby sighed. "Just an incomplete idea. Nobody's perfect every time." He squinted at the comic store, serious. "The dead drop is in the alley alongside the shop. Lizzie, make sure we aren't observed?"

"Sure, boss," she said, still laughing.

"Hale, you come with me, I'll show you how it's done." They waited for the light to change, then casually walked across the sidewalk and ducked into the alley between the comic store and one of the fancy clothing boutiques.

"Why'd she call you boss?"

He laughed. "Because she likes to tease me. We take turns running things when we're working together. If we're doing surveillance or gathering intel, I take charge. I'm better at those. I'm better at... details. When we're breaking into a heavily guarded compound or running away, she takes the lead. She's a lot better at, you know, the physical stuff." He patted his round stomach knowingly. "Ah, here we go."

Filby pointed to a big trash bin, so rusty you could catch tetanus just looking at it. He went to the far side of the bin and knelt down. "There's a loose brick here," he said, running his finger down the bricks in the wall, counting under his breath. "Ah ha."

Jake glanced down the alley and gasped. He grabbed Filby's arm. "Look!"

One of the blond twins from the park was at the far end of the alley, trying to act like he was just strolling by — at least until he saw Jake and Filby looking at him. Then he grinned and started down the alleyway toward them.

"They must have followed us from the park," Filby cursed. "This drop is blown, we've got to go!" He thrust the small metal case with the test tube and the dead bee at Jake. "Run," he whispered. "Meet us at the safe house where you saw Lizzie, at six o'clock, and make sure you aren't followed."

Then Filby grabbed onto the trash bin's handle and pulled — the bin was huge, and heavy, but it was on wheels, and once Filby heaved on it a couple of times it started to slide around sideways, completely blocking the alley. "Go, now! I'll slow him down!"

Jake ran, not looking back to see what Filby was doing, the test tube clutched to his chest. He burst out of the alleyway, startling Lizzie.

"What's wrong?" she gasped.

"You've got something that doesn't belong to you," the other blond kid said, appearing from around the corner. "Do me a favor, and don't give it up without a fight. I love a—"

Lizzie dropped, spun, and kicked the bully's legs out from under him. He fell with a shout and a squawk, landing on his butt so hard Jake winced in involuntary sympathy.

"Run, new kid," Lizzie said, settling into a stance that looked vaguely like something from a martial arts movie. "I've got this."

Jake hesitated just a moment before he shoved the bee into a pocket of his cargo shorts. He grabbed his bike, then saw Lizzie's red one and grabbed that instead. She would forgive him. He took off pedaling in the direction her bike happened to be pointed. After his clunky, heavy old three-speed, riding this one felt like flying through the air. He put his head down and pedaled harder, thinking.

Okay: there were enemy agents in the area. At least two. They'd followed them from the park, so they shouldn't know who Jake actually was, or where he lived, or even about the safe house on Gleam Street.

How could Jake make sure he wasn't followed back to either of those places, though? He'd been riding his bike around town for years, so he knew lots of shortcuts, and they weren't even after him right now. Filby and Lizzie were probably keeping them plenty busy —

A bike came flying out of a side street, the blond bully driving it almost colliding with Jake. He lost some speed when he had to slow down to turn his bike in the same direction as Jake's, but he was in pursuit seconds later, and worst of all, he was laughing as he pedaled, like Jake even trying to escape him was the funniest thing in the world.

EVASION AND ESCAPE

Jake cut through an alley, zooming through barriers that kept cars out, then jumped his bike off the curb and pedaled furiously in the direction of Angleton Park. There were lots of forest trails near there, and if this kid wasn't local, there was no way he'd be able to keep up with Jake there.

But the blond was bigger, and stronger, and pedaling faster, and as Jake raced flat-out, he heard the constant laughter behind him grow closer and louder. He glanced at the rearview mirror on the handlebars and saw his pursuer reach into a pocket and draw out a slim black cylinder with his right hand. The boy flicked his wrist, and the cylinder expanded, telescoping out into a rod about three feet long, with a metal ball at one end. Then the boy twisted something on the baton's handle, and needle-sharp spikes sprouted from the ball. The boy swung the spiked baton at the back of Jake's bike — he was trying to pop the rear tire!

Jake looked away from the mirror, back at the world in front of him, and realized he was approaching a stoplight at an intersection — and the light was red. Jake could hardly stop, not with this kid behind him, but he wasn't about to risk flying through the intersection and getting walloped by a truck. So he yanked his handlebars, turning as sharply as he dared, and jumped his front wheel up onto the sidewalk, which — fortunately — was free of women pushing strollers or men pushing strollers or anyone walking dogs. He turned the corner hard, staying on the sidewalk until the end of the block, then veered back onto the street.

The kid behind him was steering one-handed, so he couldn't whip around into a turn as fast as Jake could, which widened the gap between them. But Jake's legs were starting to burn, and the kid grew larger in the rearview. He wasn't laughing anymore. He was scowling, and baring his teeth, and standing up on the bike, pedaling hard. Jake wasn't going to make it to the park and the trails. He'd be caught long before then — and what would this kid do when he caught him?

But Jake realized he was thinking like a scared kid, instead of like a Stormglass agent. The bike had evasion countermeasures, right? He fumbled with the panel on the handlebars, finally getting it open, and looking at the unmarked glowing buttons inside. Caltrops, oil slick, motor... but he couldn't actually remember which button did what.

Another glance at the mirror showed the boy, spiked club in hand, getting dangerously close to striking range again. Anything at all would be helpful now, so he smacked the button farthest to the right and hoped for the best.

The bike surged forward, moving so fast he almost fell off the back, and he clung to the handlebars as hard as he could with both hands. The whole bike vibrated, and the motor hidden under the seat let out a steady buzz.

The boy chasing Jake actually howled, like a predator watching the prey it wanted for dinner get away, and Jake grinned as the wind whipped past him, blowing so hard it brought tears to his eyes. He was free! He was okay!

Except this particular road ended at a t-shaped intersection — now rapidly approaching — and Jake was going too fast to turn in either direction. If he kept going forward, he'd hit the tree-filled field where this road dead-ended, and that wasn't good, either. The kid behind him was a fading dot, so Jake gripped the brakes, which didn't seem to do much of anything to slow him down. He pressed the button again, which cut off the buzz of the motor, but he was still going way too fast. The brakes seemed to make a difference, but not enough –

Jake suddenly wished he'd had the sense to wear his helmet.

The bike sailed through the intersection and cut into the bumpy, grassy field beyond. He held on and managed to stay upright and rolling, but dense redwood trees were looming up fast. Jake had no choice: he threw himself sideways.

He skidded into the grass, the rough soil ripping at his shirt and jeans, the impact knocking the wind out of him. As he slowed to a halt, he looked up at the tree branches above him and groaned. He wasn't really hurt, but he wasn't in a big hurry to get up, either. The bike was resting half on top of him, the back wheel on top of his legs, one of his hands still holding the handlebars.

"Gotcha," the blond said, and Jake was so surprised to hear the voice he gasped out loud. The blond hadn't stopped chasing him, but he had stopped laughing, allowing him to leave his bike and creep up on Jake on foot.

"Give me the bee, right now," the boy said, "and I'll just break one of your legs." He still held the baton with the spiked tip in his hand, and he whipped it through the air a few times, making a nasty little whooshing sound.

"Okay," Jake said. "Just don't hurt me, I don't even want to work for Stormglass, this is stupid, I thought it was a game—"

The blond stepped closer, crouching down near Jake's feet. "Whining. I hate whining. First I'm going to break your leg. Then I'm going to break your ankle — the ankle on the other leg."

Jake pressed one of the other buttons on the handlebars, and a compartment on the back wheel popped open. Nothing very dramatic happened, though: a few dozen shiny metal objects fell out onto the grass. They looked a lot like the metal spikes from jacks, though much pointier. The blond boy laughed. "Those would have worked great if you'd used them when I was chasing you, idiot, but they're not much good now—"

Jake hit the other button.

The results were much more impressive this time. A small hose, tipped with a nozzle, was attached to the back of his bike, and it sprayed a torrent of sticky black goo right into the blond boy's face, including into his open mouth. He gagged, shouted, and fell backward, as more goo sprayed all around him, the club falling from his hand.

Jake grinned. The oily slime made a decent projectile weapon, too. After a couple of seconds the slime reservoir was empty, and Jake hurried to his feet, hauling his bike up after him. The blond was wiping at his eyes, cursing, spitting, and crawling around blindly, but he kept slipping on the oily grass and going facedown into the dirt.

Pausing only to snatch up the kid's ugly baton, Jake ran the bike as fast as he could back out to the road. The blond boy's bike was there, and Jake slashed down at both tires with the spiked club, popping them. He just left the baton sticking out of the back tire — he couldn't imagine actually trying to bike while holding onto the thing. If he crashed and fell on it, he'd put his own eyes out.

"You don't mess with us!" the blond shouted through the oil in a muffled, choking voice. "We never let people mess with us!"

Jake didn't hear the rest, because he was pedaling away as fast as he possibly could.

UNSAFE HOUSE

After a while, satisfied that he was wasn't being followed, Jake pedaled more sedately toward his house, tucking Lizzie's bike out of sight in the garage when he arrived, and went straight up to his room. He sat in his desk chair for a few minutes, taking deep breaths as his body trembled, the last of the adrenaline and whatever other panic-and-excitement chemicals his body had produced leaving his system.

Once he'd calmed down, he realized there was nothing to do but wait. He opened up his computer, which was really his dad's old laptop, and launched a web browser. But when he typed 'Stormglass' into a search engine, he didn't find much. There were lots of pages about an old weather-predicting device, and some about the game, but there was nothing about a real crime-fighting organization. That made sense though, if it was all super-secret.

He searched for 'Lizzie Lew' and one of the first pages was about a Civil War spy from Virginia. That probably explained where Lizzie had gotten her code name. Jake wondered if she'd chosen it herself, or been assigned it, the way he'd been stuck with the name Hale. Then he searched for 'Hale,' and found an old war hero who was captured by the British and hanged. That wasn't very encouraging. Jake scrolled down the page. The man's last words were, "I only regret that I have but one life to give for my country."

A search on 'Filby' didn't turn up anything, really. It was a common last name, and a town in England. Maybe Filby came from there. He sure didn't sound English, but weren't some secret agents good at doing fake accents?

Jake tried a few lines in a fake English accent, but it sounded terrible, so he then tried Scottish, Indian, and Australian, but decided he needed a lot more practice before he used any of them as anything other than a joke.

Eventually, though, he ran out of things to think about, and started worrying about Filby and Lizzie instead. What if one of them had been captured? Only one of the twins had gone after him, which left one of them to go after his friends. But they were seasoned secret agents, right? Lizzie seemed like she could fight her way out of just about any situation, and Filby was probably smart enough to escape. Surely they could get away from the other twin when it was two-against-one.

He decided the time was close enough. He'd get to the house on Gleam Street early, but he could always climb the tree and wait if he needed to. He went downstairs and called to his dad, "I'm going outside for a little while! I'll be back for dinner!"

His dad yelled back something unintelligible, but it didn't sound like a refusal, so Jake checked to make sure he had the bee and his HyperOpticon and started for the front door.

Then he had an idea, and spent a few minutes digging through the drawers in one corner of the living room. His parents were always working their craft projects, and there were drawers full of modeling clay, wires, fuzzy pipe cleaners, and other junk. He spent a few minutes on his spur-of-the-moment project, decided it was good enough, and then set out for the house on Gleam Street.

He walked, because that was slower and he had time to kill. Jake kept his eyes peeled for anyone suspicious, and took a long and roundabout route, going a few blocks out of his way and ducking behind hedges and rows of garbage cans lined up at the curb, just to be safe. He thought he was getting pretty good at this secret agent stuff. If it was actually for real, that is.

When he rounded the corner on Gleam Street, there was a guy leaning against a light pole on the corner, squinting at a folded street map. Jake was instantly suspicious, because there was nothing much of interest in this neighborhood.

The guy didn't look anything like a criminal, though. He looked like he was in his twenties, and he wore jeans and a blue polo shirt — totally ordinary. Jake decided to ignore him — or pretend to ignore him — and crossed to the other side of the street. Maybe the twins had captured and interrogated Lizzie and Filby, and knew about the house on Gleam Street. Better to play it safe. He could circle back home and wait for Lizzie and Filby to contact him.

Jake continued walking along the sidewalk for a while, then glanced backward. The guy was walking his direction, looking down at his map, but keeping pace with Jake.

Uh oh.

Jake veered right at the next corner, and halfway down the block, he glanced back. The guy was still coming. Jake stopped, smacked himself on the forehead, and said out loud, "How could I forget that!" Then he started walking back the way he'd come. The guy reading the map held it up close to his face, shook his head, sighed, and turned to walk back in the same direction Jake was going, as if he'd just realized he'd been going the wrong way too.

Crud. Jake was scared now, and wasn't sure what to do. Go knock on somebody's door and tell them a strange man was following him? That could work — most of his neighbors would call the cops right away, or at least confront the guy and chase him off. He started for the nearest house with light in the windows, a one-story with brown shingle walls, and hurried up the steps. He rang the doorbell, but heard nothing, so started banging on the door. He started hitting it harder, and harder, and realized with a sinking feeling in his gut that no one was coming.

He turned, and the man was standing at the bottom of the steps, smiling up at him in a friendly way. This close, Jake could see the thick white scar that ran all the way from his forehead to his chin.

"I'll scream if you come any closer," Jake said.

The guy looked surprised. "Why would you do that? I'm from Stormglass. I went to check the dead drop, but the location was compromised. So I'm here to pick up whatever you and Lizzie and Filby found."

"Lizzie told me that if an adult ever said they were a Stormglass agent, not to believe them."

The man chuckled. "Do I look that old? It wasn't so long ago that I was a new agent, too. It's good for you to be suspicious. That's exactly what we look for in a young agent. But when a dead drop has been blown, things change quickly. I'm sure you understand."

"What's the secret sign?"

The man shook his head. "Come on, boy. We don't have time for games and secret handshakes. This is important—"

"What's my name, then?" Jake asked. "Or even my code name?"

The guy hesitated for just a second. "I don't think it's a good idea to mention names out here in public—"

"You didn't mind mentioning Filby and Lizzie." Jake crossed his arms over his chest. "I'm not giving you anything. Who do you work for? Vindiqo?"

"Oh, now don't be ridiculous."

"If you don't turn around and walk away in the next five seconds, I'm going to scream my head off," Jake said. "Five. Four. Three—"

The man reached into his pocket and came out with a small black gun, which he held close to his body. "You might want to stop counting now," he said, and his voice was no longer friendly at all.

ENEMY ENCOUNTER

Jake stared at the gun. He'd never seen a real pistol up close before, and he was amazed at how much it didn't look like a toy. It was metal, and black, and solid, and it looked heavy. There was a tube screwed onto the end of the barrel.

"Ah, you've noticed the noise suppressor," the guy with the scar running down his face said. "People call them 'silencers,' sometimes, but that's not right. You can't actually silence a gun. You can only muffle the noise. When I fire the gun, you'd only hear a very loud cough."

The guy, who clearly wasn't a Stormglass agent, took a step closer, and looked at Jake, his expression utterly blank. "Actually, you wouldn't hear anything. You'd be dead. I'd normally threaten to crush your windpipe — my favorite method of murder — but I'm in a hurry today. I've been given a job: recover the bee. So how about you hand the dead bug over, and we can both get on with our lives?"

Jake swallowed, then nodded. He reached into his pocket and removed the metal case. He thought about doing something crazy — throwing it at the guy's face and dodging out of the way — but... there was a gun. You don't mess around with guys who have guns.

The man snatched the package, and fumblingly opened the case with one hand, keeping the gun pointed in Jake's general direction the whole time. He glanced at the yellow-and-black shape inside the test tube, nodded once, and shoved the vial in his pocket. "See?" he said. "No fuss, no problems. Listen, boy. Let me give you a piece of advice. This is no line of work for children. Go ride your bike, build your tree fort, and set up your lemonade stand on the sidewalk. Don't mess around with Stormglass, and don't mess around with Vindiqo. Leave it to the grown-ups. We know what's best for you. Let us worry about the future."

Jake opened his mouth — he wanted to say something like, "But I'm the one who has to live in that future, you jerk" — but this guy still had the gun, so he just nodded.

"Good boy." The man turned on his heel and strode quickly away toward the west, sliding the pistol back into his jacket.

Jake leaned against the door and let out a breath he hadn't even realized he'd been holding, his whole body shaking. He couldn't remember when he'd been so scared before — not even when the blond boy had threatened to break his ankle — and he'd certainly never been scared for a better reason. After a few minutes spent taking deep breaths and trying to get himself under control, his racing heartbeat slowed down, and he started to feel normal again.

He stood upright and padded slowly down the steps, looking around and worrying about what he should do. Clearly the house on Gleam Street was known about by whoever these people were, but he didn't have any other plan. So he decided to just go home where it was safe, and wait.

He walked back home without seeing anyone suspicious, or anyone else at all, apart from a stray cat that ran underneath a car to hide from him. Jake could relate.

But when he got home and opened the front door, Jake found his living room was crowded. His mom was there, and his dad, and Lizzie and Filby too! They were sitting side by side on the couch. "There you are," his mom said, smiling. "We were just talking to your new friends."

"Oh, hi, guys," Jake said, trying to hide his surprise. "I thought we were going to meet, uh, someplace else?"

"Yeah, sorry," Filby said. "We were hoping we could catch you here. Before you left."

"I've asked your friends if they want to stay for dinner," his mom said, walking over and kissing him on top of the head — *gah, so embarrassing!*

"We'd love to," Lizzie said.

"It's just pasta and salad," Jake's dad said, "but we've got lots."

They all hung around in the kitchen while Jake's dad boiled water and his mom mixed up the salad. His parents were basically in full-on friendly interrogation mode, asking Lizzie and Filby when they'd moved to town (just a couple of weeks ago), what their parents did (antiques dealer and security consultant, so they traveled a lot), whether they played any sports (Lizzie played field hockey, and Filby asked if they considered chess a sport). Everyone was so relaxed and chatty and friendly that Jake found himself relaxing, too, and Lizzie and Filby were just like normal kids, a pair of stepsiblings cracking jokes and being silly. He wondered how much of that was an act, and how much was real — just them having the chance to stop acting like secret agents for a little while.

It must be very confusing to be an agent, he decided. It would be hard to tell which parts of your life were real. Maybe they were all real.

They all sat down for dinner together — the dining room table actually got cleaned off entirely, for the first time in months — and while they were working through their pasta and salad, Jake's dad said, "So I hear you kids are secret agents."

Jake froze with his fork halfway to his mouth, looking at Lizzie and Filby, but they didn't react strangely at all. "Yeah, we're going to have to talk to Jake after dinner to give him a secret briefing," Filby said. "If that's okay."

"Oh, sure," Jake's dad said. "But there's also chocolate ice cream for dessert. I hope ice cream won't interfere with your briefing."

"Some things are more important than the fate of the world," Filby said. "If we skip eating ice cream because we're too busy fighting, what are we even fighting for?"

STORMGADGETS

"Your parents are cool!" Lizzie spun around and around in Jake's swivel desk chair, while Filby ran a glowing cellphone-sized gadget across electrical outlets, light fixtures, lamps, and computers, sweeping everything for listening devices or hidden cameras.

"They're okay," Jake said. "I'm just glad you two are all right. How'd you get away from the other twin at the dead drop?"

"Evasion and concealment," Filby said.

"By which he means, running and hiding," Lizzie laughed.

"Running and hiding is nothing to be ashamed about," Filby said, "at least not under those circumstances. We made it to the safe house on Gleam Street, and saw it was under surveillance, too — I don't know how they found that location. Maybe they've been watching us for longer than I thought. Those twins..." He shook his head. "They're scary guys."

"I made some calls," Lizzie said, "and they're definitely the same twins from the photo. They're just a little older than us, working for Vindiqo. They look so bland, like any country club jerks, just more psychotic. Um, Hale, you know my bike was taking pictures during that whole chase, right?"

Jake blinked twice, then suddenly remembered the small camera mounted on the handlebars.

"It uploaded them while it was all happening," Lizzie said. "I can't believe you got away from that creepo twin!"

"For a new kid," Filby said, "You're catching on pretty quick."

"Oh, I've got your old bike," Lizzie said, pausing mid-spin in the chair. "I rode it back here. I don't know how you stand the thing — it was like riding an arthritic camel. So did anything else happen?"

"Well, I had my first gun pointed at me," Jake said. Both Filby and Lizzie's eyes opened wide. They knew there was a good story coming.

"Report," Filby said, and Jake quickly told them about the guy with the scar on his face.

"He pretended to be a Stormglass agent."

Lizzie whistled. "Did he really? You didn't believe him, though? Man, to threaten you out in public, with a gun? They must really want the bee back! Did you hand it over?"

"It's okay if you did," Filby said. "Only fight someone with a gun if you're sure you're going to die. It's better to just do what he says."

Jake grinned. "Well, maybe I was a little crazy." He reached into his pocket and removed a rolled-up plastic bag, which he unfolded to reveal the bee. "I gave him a fake bee, but I guess it looked real enough!"

Lizzie laughed and gave him a high five. "The switcheroo! Nicely done, new kid!" she said.

Filby nodded. "Yes. Quick thinking and improvisation. Very good counterespionage. It might be a good idea to avoid active operations so close to your home, though, at least for a while. We don't want you to draw attention to yourself."

Jake slumped on the bed when he heard this. He'd only just joined, and was already being told he couldn't investigate anymore.

"Really? I don't get to work with you guys anymore? I went to a lot of trouble to keep hold of that bee – I want to know what's going on!"

"Oh, you can still work with us," Lizzie said with a mysterious smile. "Just not around here. You showed some quick thinking today. You're ready to level up."

Filby nodded. "We've been authorized to give you the rest of your kit now." He pulled a black backpack out from under Jake's bed. When had he hidden that? Filby heaved the backpack up onto the bed. "Here's your first set of Stormgadgets." He unzipped the backpack, then stepped back so Jake could take a look.

The backpack was full of pockets, shaped just right to fit the objects inside, and arranged for maximum space efficiency. There was an empty pocket for the HyperOpticon, but the other pockets held unknown devices, all black plastic and dark metal, shining wire and gleaming screens.

Filby gestured at several in quick succession. "UV scanner. Useful for detecting fingerprints, bloodstains, stuff like that. Night vision goggles to see in the dark. This miniature spy camera streams video to the cloud, and these little buttons are magnetic listening devices, sound-activated. It covers all the spy basics. Whereas this..." He lifted out a small tablet, the size of a paperback book. "This is your Stormpad, Hale."

Filby handed the metal-cased tablet to Jake.

"Like an iPad?" Jake asked as he took the Stormpad. It weighed almost nothing, and felt cool and smooth in his hands. *This is awesome*, he thought.

"Nothing like it," Filby said. "It's a virtual crime lab, digital dead drop, back-channel untraceable communications device, and online encyclopedia. You can use it to tune in to police radio and other emergency frequencies."

"Plus, it talks," Lizzie said. "It can carry on a pretty good conversation. I call it Stormy."

"Wow," Jake said. "That's awesome... I can't wait to play with this. So can I contact you guys with this?"

Filby nodded. "Sure, but you can also review case files and get support in the field. If you need blueprints, or want to get the security cameras in a building shut down for a couple of minutes, or need to trigger an alarm system somewhere, use this."

"We do get some good tools," nodded Lizzie.

"But remember Hale," said Filby, "Being an agent is about more than gadgets."

"Watch the world in a different way," said Lizzie, "and find the tools you need to survive. Sometimes you just need a rock, a shoe, a piece of broken glass, the kindness of a stranger, or a single scream in a crowded place. Think fast, improvise, and always be ready to adapt. Which you've already done. The fake bee, getting away from those crazy twins, you're showing promise."

Filby nodded. "It's a good start. With a little training, you'll be even better. Just don't forget, the most valuable gadget is your brain, followed closely by your instincts." He paused. "And yes, farther down the list are things like stun guns and grappling hooks.

"And jetpacks," added Lizzie.

"She's kidding," Filby said. "We don't have jetpacks."

"Yet!"

Jake laughed, and zipped up the backpack. "So what happens next?"

"We've transmitted photos of the bee to headquarters, and they're analyzing them," Filby said. "And since you've kept ahold of the bee, I guess we'll see what happens. Keep it safe."

"And stay away from the house on Gleam Street," Lizzie said. "We'll be in touch."

Jake walked them downstairs, where they thanked his parents for dinner, and refused the offer of a ride home — Jake suddenly wondered where they were sleeping, since their safe house had been compromised. Maybe they had a backup location somewhere, or maybe they were just "improvising."

He walked outside with them to retrieve Lizzie's bike. She grumbled, "You'd better hope I don't have to escape from anyone when I'm riding this thing tonight. You used up all my gadgets!"

"Improvise," Jake said with a smirk. "Throw a shoe at them. Or the kindness of a stranger."

Lizzie stuck her tongue out at him as she climbed on the bike, and he watched them pedal off into the darkness.

"Those are nice kids," his mom said. "I'm glad you met them, since so many of your school friends are gone this summer."

"I might have to go with them to do some secret agent stuff tomorrow," Jake said. "I'm not sure yet. It could take a while."

"I'm sure we can arrange for you to do a sleepover at their house if you like," his dad said. *Sleepover. Right.*

THE TRAITOR (1)

Once they were safely ensconced in the ruins of an abandoned ice skating rink — an even less inviting safe house than the one on Gleam Street — the traitor found an excuse to slip away.

The traitor couldn't use a Stormpad to contact Vindiqo, of course, because the transmission would be tracked, and recorded, and logged somewhere in the humming computerized heart of Stormglass headquarters. So the traitor used a special smartphone, hidden and untraceable.

When the screen lit up, it briefly flashed a stylized V, then switched to video chat. The traitor smiled, because the face on the screen wasn't the cold and unsympathetic Mundt, but the familiar and kind features of the Doctor himself.

"Is your position secure?" the Doctor asked. "Where is your partner?"

"Keeping watch," the traitor whispered. "In another room. I can't talk for long..."

"Mmm. How did the day go?" the Doctor said, and then laughed. "Another glorious Stormglass success?"

"You didn't tell me the twins and Mundt were going to show up. I almost didn't recognize them."

"But you did. You're smart. Smarter than people realize. And that's why you're such an outstanding resource."

"What about the bee? Did you leave that in the park on purpose? I mean, you even had a Vindiqo logo printed on it—"

"Ah, yes — the bee. That was a little gift for old Cyrus Rex," the Doctor said. "Make sure he gets it, won't you? I would like him to be interested in them."

"He's already hooked. But, do the twins or Mundt know about me," the traitor said. "Just in case."

"Mundt does, but the boys? Of course not."

"So if I see the twins in the field, they'll be dangerous... I mean, I can defend myself — but they could have killed the others!"

"They're spirited boys," the Doctor said, as if agreeing with the traitor. "Oh, they're spirited boys alright. But you're able to take care of yourself. You always have. I knew you'd escape them. This new recruit impressed me, as well! I didn't expect him to get away or outsmart Mundt, and he did both. It's put dear Mundt in a terrible mood. He's been smashing holes in the walls with his mechanical hand all evening. It's so tiring. But this new agent reminds me a little of you, with some obvious differences of course. I wonder if he might be interested in meeting with me? Hmmm."

The Doctor leaned back in his chair and popped open a can of Splurge Soda before continuing, "Yes, we'll deal with that later. You know what to do at

Stormglass, of course? You still have the files? You'll be able to deposit them at the headquarters?"

The traitor frowned. "Yes, yes, but it's going to be tricky. Security is so tight…"

"Ah, and that's why I'm so happy you're on our side. I've never seen someone who can keep you out. Together, my friend, you and I will make the world a better place. And get furiously rich doing it."

The traitor sighed, happily. "And who could ask for anything more?"

MEET STORM

After saying his goodnights and shutting his door, Jake climbed into bed with his Stormpad. He plugged in his headphones and popped the earbuds in, then powered up the machine.

The touchscreen showed a blue glowing handprint, which Jake automatically pressed his palm against. It pulsed with bluish light and then chimed.

"Welcome to Stormglass, Hale."

Jake's eyes widened.

"Uh, is this... the computer?" *Could it hear him?*

"Affirmative," said the voice.

"Really?"

"Please stand by for audio recording from Echelon Leader."

"Agent Hale, you never know when you'll have to spring into action," she said. "Sleep when you can. That's your first spy lesson, and I'm giving it to you free."

"Okay," Jake said, although he realized he was talking to a message. "Goodnight, Storm." He felt even more ridiculous saying that to a computer, but the Stormpad actually replied, "Powering down." The screen went blank.

Jake stowed the Stormpad in his desk, then climbed back into bed. He really needed to sleep... but he was practically vibrating with excitement.

His summer was suddenly getting a whole lot better.

FIELD TRIP

The next morning Jake woke up later than usual, and the first thing he did was take out his Stormpad. After he activated it with his handprint, the screen flashed "Message waiting," and popped up a little envelope icon. Jake tapped it, and a video began running: Filby's face in close-up, mostly hidden in shadow.

"Good morning, Hale," he said. "We've received details about our next mission. Congratulations, you're going back into the field. We're meeting with a retired Stormglass agent, an entomologist."

Lizzie stuck her face in front of the camera, "That's a bug guy to you and me. Who knew Stormglass even had a bug guy?"

Hale pushed her away. "Come on Lizzie, this message is supposed to sound official!" He turned back to the screen, and said, "Be ready to leave on short notice, don't forget the package, and bring a jacket – England is cold."

Jake just stared at his Stormpad. He was supposed to go to England? He'd never been out of the country — the farthest he'd ever gone from home was a vacation in Hawaii with his parents! There was no way his mom and dad would give him permission to take a plane across the ocean with kids he just met, and he didn't want to lie to them.

He went downstairs, where his dad was making one of his epic Saturday breakfasts, with bacon and scrambled eggs and sausage and fresh-squeezed orange juice and raggedy-edged waffles. His mom was home. A lot of weekends she had to travel for work, but not this time. She was sitting at the dining room table, reading one of the free weekly newspapers. "Look who decided to wake up!" she said.

"He was tired from all that crime-fighting yesterday," his dad said from the stove, poking bacon and making it hiss.

"Speaking of your new friends," his mom said, "I got a call from Filby's mother this morning, asking if you could go to their lake house for a few days. Why didn't you tell us they'd invited you?"

"Huh?" Jake said.

"It's fine with us if you want to go," his dad said. "Just keep your phone on in case we need to reach you, and be sure to call us when you get there." He shook his head. "I wonder what it was like for Filby, going from being an only child to having a step-sister almost his own age? My big sister always annoyed me, and I knew her my whole life."

Jake realized his parents knew more about Lizzie and Filby's fake cover identities than he did.

"Filby's dad was on to something, marrying a woman with a lake house," his mom said. "Why don't we have a lake house? I could go for a week of hanging out in the country."

"The woods never have a good internet connection," his dad said, and shuddered. "I can't deal with that."

His mom snorted. "You used to go camping all the time when we met. You've gone soft."

Jake thought for a moment. Nobody had told him he had to lie to his parents. How could you live that kind of secret life, with the people you were closest to? He didn't like the idea of being dishonest — especially about something this big — so he said, "I'm pretty sure there's no lake house. I think I'm actually flying to England to meet a secret agent bee expert guy."

"Ah, an entomologist! Didn't Sherlock Holmes become a beekeeper when he quit being a detective?" his dad said. "I think I remember reading that. Keep an eye out for him, okay?"

Jake sighed, and tried again. "And whoever you talked to, they probably weren't really Filby's mom. I'd guess they were another secret agent."

"Well, that makes sense," his mom said. "Secret agents usually ask a lot of questions about the best farmers' markets in the area, in my experience. You know, deadly spy tomatoes and all that."

"Aren't you even a little worried that I'm actually running off to England?" Jake said.

"You don't even have a passport," his mom said with a laugh. "So, no, I can't say I'm too concerned."

A passport! Good point. Though Stormglass could probably work around things like that.

"All this secret agent stuff reminds me of college, Jake," his dad said. "That's how your mom and I met, we played this game where you pretended to be a spy and someone would slip secret missions under your door. You never really knew who was playing, and the game never stopped, so you'd get really paranoid walking around campus. If you weren't careful, some enemy agent would shoot you with a squirt gun or slip hot sauce into your coffee — that was 'poison' — and then you were out of the game. Your mom nailed me with a water-balloon bomb from her window when I was on my way to class. It was love at first splash."

"Your dad was pretty good, though," his mom remembered. "They called him The Trapdoor Spider, because he was so patient. He'd just lie in wait until the perfect moment, and then strike."

"Really?" Jake said. "You guys played that?"

"Your mom was The Black Widow. So deadly," his dad said, and looked over at his mom with a nostalgic smile. "Those were some good times. I guess being a secret agent is in your blood, Jake."

"Okay," Jake said. "I'll pack a bag for the trip, then."

Lizzie called on Jake's home phone around noon. "It's go time," she said. "Meet us at the corner of Elm and Ash."

Jake told his parents he was going over to meet Lizzie and Filby, but declined when they offered to drive him over — "It's just a couple of blocks, and I like walking" — and said his farewells. Jake strapped on the bulging backpack that contained his Stormglass gear and some extra clothes and set off for the rendezvous point, keeping his eyes open for the twins or the guy with the facial scar.

At Elm and Ash, a black sedan parked at the curb started its engine as he approached. The back door swung open and Lizzie poked her head out. "Stick your bag in the trunk and slide on in," she said.

Jake stowed his bag, slammed the trunk shut, and climbed into the back seat with Filby and Lizzie. Filby didn't even say hello, concentrating intensely on his Stormpad instead. A bored-looking driver sat up front.

"Drive on," Lizzie said once Jake had his seatbelt on. "Car service," she explained. "Very discreet, does a lot of work for the agency. He'll take us to the plane."

"Which airport are we going to? There's an In-N-Out Burger by the Oakland Airport, maybe we could stop for—"

Filby groaned. "Mmmm… In-N-Out. Now all I can think about is a triple double burger, animal style."

"No burgers for you boys," Lizzie said. "We're not taking off from a normal airport, Hale. They're not so discreet, you know? There's a little airstrip not far from here that hardly gets used any more."

"So we're taking a private plane?"

"Yeah," Lizzie said. "But a boring one. Like a Cessna business jet, the kind rich bankers use. It's too bad, because we have a lot of cool—"

Filby cleared his throat loudly and then pressed a button on his door that raised a black glass partition between them and the driver's seat. "Okay," Filby said. "Now you can gush about flying machines, but nothing above his security clearance, all right?"

Lizzie grinned. "If you go to headquarters, Hale – when, I should probably say — I'll take you to the hangar. It's awesome. We've got the only working models of some amazing experimental aircraft. A Bell X-2 Starbuster, a Proteus, a Fairey Rotodyne…"

Hale raised one eyebrow comically. "A roto-what?"

"It's like a helicopter, if a helicopter was the Incredible Hulk," continued Lizzie, "and a Nord 1500 Ramjet and a Hafner Rotobuggy, and then there are all the—"

"Any of this making sense to you, Hale?" said Filby.

"I heard the word helicopter," Hale said. "And the Incredible Hulk. So, a green helicopter?"

"You two have no appreciation for the wonders of aeronautic engineering," Lizzie said with a harrumph, folding her arms and sitting back.

"And she's the one who gives the big speech about how you don't need gadgets," Filby said.

Lizzie stuck out her tongue. "Anyway, Hale, we're not taking one of those. We're stuck with something a little more boring."

"So now I've got the kind of life," Jake said slowly, "where taking a private plane to England is boring?"

"It only gets more interesting from here," Filby promised.

FIRST FLIGHT

The airfield looked more like a farm than an airport: just a cleared space among the trees, with a couple of sheet metal buildings, and a little shack with a tall antenna tower. A gleaming white plane waited on the runway, stairs folded down and ready for them to board. Jake followed Lizzie and Filby up the steps into the plane, and stopped in the doorway, just staring.

He'd been on airplanes before, visiting relatives and going on vacation, but this was nothing like a commercial plane — it looked more like a comfy living room, with couches and brown leather armchairs and plush carpeting, real wooden tables, and even a couple of flat-screen televisions running along one wall.

"Come on," Lizzie said. "I know it's cool, but you'll get used to it." When he moved out of the doorway, she pulled up the stairs and then tugged a big lever to seal the aircraft door. Filby was already sitting at one of the tables, working on his Stormpad. Lizzie went up front and banged on the closed cockpit door. The planes engines started to hum.

Jake lowered himself onto the couch, which felt more comfortable than the one in his own house. "So that's it? We just... take off now?"

"Yep," said Filby. He looked out the window and shrugged. "Not much traffic."

Lizzie sprawled on the couch beside Jake. "This is how the rich live," she said. "Pretty perfect, huh? Enjoy it while you can – life at Stormglass isn't always this good. More often we end up in the back of a truck full of beets, or hiding under stinky blankets in the belly of a ship. Somebody must be worried about this bee. They want us to get it to the bug guy, fast."

"How long until we get to England?" Jake said.

"Eight or ten hours?" Lizzie said. "I forget." She looked at Filby, who was usually happy to correct her, but he was engrossed in something on his Stormpad. So she shrugged. "A pretty long time, anyway. Should we see what kind of DVDs they've got here? Might as well do a little film festival."

"Really? Don't you need to, I don't know, practice taking a gun apart and putting it back together, or do a thousand push-ups or something?"

"Ha," she laughed. "We don't use guns. We aren't assassins — we're the good guys."

"What about the time you shot the butler?" asked Filby, momentarily popping his head up before diving back into his Stormpad.

"Okay, okay. We don't use guns," she repeated, then increased her speed dramatically, "except-for-that-one-lousy-time-I-shot-a-butler-with-a-tranquilizer-dart. But I really had to, and... well... thanks, Filby."

"Okay, forget the guns, shouldn't we be, like, studying maps of England or learning about bee... thoraxes, or whatever..."

Lizzie shrugged. "Sure, but Filby's doing enough of that for both of us. Being a secret agent on the go is stressful, Hale, so relax when you can. You were held at gunpoint yesterday. Why not watch an action movie or two?"

"I could go for that," Jake said with a big smile, and sank back into the cushions.

Three movies, a couple of sandwiches, and a long nap later, the plane landed in darkness, bumping Jake into consciousness. "Wha?" He blinked around the dim interior of the plane.

"We're here," Filby said, still sitting at the table with his Stormpad — had he moved during the trip? "England. Hip hip, cheerio, and God Save the Queen. Tea and crumpets. Soccer, but they call it football. Uh. Redcoats? Crown jewels? I'm reaching the limits of my British knowledge."

"Are you still working?" Jake said, rubbing his eyes.

"Sure, if breaking my record in *Temple Run* counts as working," Filby said. "Come on, Hale. I'm not a robot!"

MELLIFERA HALL

Jake laughed, yawned again, and stretched out his arms asking, "What time is it anyway?"

Lizzie snorted. "It's like four in the morning here. Let's see how well you cope with a little jetlag, Hale. But wait until you fly to Australia and have to literally hit the ground running."

"Literally hit the ground running?" Filby said with one raised eyebrow. "Hopefully you mean figuratively, unless you're predicting a nasty fall for our friend Hale."

Lizzie frowned. "Figuratively, literally, whatever — grab your gear, guys! Our ride awaits."

They stepped off the plane into a dark field, brightened only by the blinking runway lights — which winked off moments after Jake's feet hit the ground. The air was cold, clear, and a little damp, and the stars above were so bright. They were like the lights of a city viewed from the sky. Oakland never had this many stars, did it?

Jake tightened the straps of his backpack more comfortably on his shoulders and waited for his eyes to adjust to the dark, but Lizzie and Filby were already striding purposefully away from the plane, bickering again, so he hurried to keep up.

A huge, ancient car — like something from an old gangster movie — sat idling beside a dirt road, the back door standing open, but with no lights on inside. They climbed in with their bags — there was plenty of room, the back seat was as wide as a sofa — and Jake pulled the door shut behind them. Jake was confused at first — there was nobody in the driver's seat, just a shadowy figure on the passenger side. Then the car started up, and Jake remembered that cars were laid out backwards in England, with the steering wheel on the passenger side. He looked out the window. Evidently they drove on the wrong side of the road, too.

It was the little things that surprised him, he thought.

The driver didn't speak, just drove, and he turned three or four times down pitch-black lanes that ran between vast fields before finally switching his headlights on. By then they were on a paved road, winding through rolling hills.

"Who is this bee guy anyway?" Jake said. He whispered, though he wasn't sure why.

"Former Stormglass agent," Lizzie said cheerfully, not whispering at all. "Old, and he knows a lot about bees. That's all that I got from the case file." She shrugged. "I guess we'll find out more when we get there."

They rode in silence, the only light in the car the illumination of Filby's Stormpad. Jake watched him for a while. The kid was astonishingly good at *Temple Run*. Though dodging monsters in pursuit was probably pretty easy for a kid who regularly escaped people like those deranged twins.

After nearly an hour in the car, the sky began to brighten, and Jake's internal sense of time complained. His body was pretty sure it was past his bedtime, but the sun seemed to think it was nearly morning. If a guy with a gun sprang out at him now, Jake didn't think he'd be able to deal with it — his brain was too fuzzy, and everything seemed sort of unreal, like he was viewing the world through dirty, warped glass. He wondered how Filby and Lizzie coped so well. Maybe they were used to it, or maybe they'd been taught special anti-jetlag techniques.

Jake was beginning to wonder if he'd ever get any training, or if he was just expected to wander around figuring things out on his own. The gadgets in his backpack were great, but he wanted somebody to show him how to use them — and to do all the other things Lizzie claimed she was able to do, too, from parachuting to disarming enemy agents. Especially since he'd had a gun aimed at him by an enemy agent. The next time that happened, he really wanted a better idea of how to cope.

He gazed out the window, and determined that England had a lot of clouds, a lot of fields, and a lot of black-and-white cows. If they didn't have time to stop at In-N-Out Burger, maybe he could convince them to take a side trip to London to see Big Ben. It might be worth a try...

Jake absentmindedly took a quarter from his pocket and started walking it across the back of his knuckles while he looked out the window, flipping the coin from one finger to another and back again. After a few moments, he noticed Filby's game had stopped, and glanced up to see both his fellow agents watching him. "What?"

"Neat trick with the coin," Lizzie said.

"It only took about a million years of practice," Jake said. He hid the coin between two of his fingers and held up a seemingly empty palm to the others. Then he held out his other hand, palm up, snapped the fingers of the hand where the coin had been hidden, and made the coin materialize from thin air, dropping into his open hand. "Ta da."

"Neat," repeated Lizzie.

"I can make a shower of coins fall out of a little kid's nose," he said laughing. "It really impresses five-year-olds."

"Misdirection and deception, quicker than the eye. That's spy smarts," Filby said.

"I never thought of it that way," Jake said.

Filby laughed and patted Jake on the shoulder. "That's the curse of being an agent," he said, "everything relates back to what we do."

"I've reached that point where I automatically scan for exits every time I enter a room," admitted Lizzie.

"And how about sitting with your back to the door?" asked Filby with a sly smile. "Would you ever do that?"

"Are you crazy? That's just begging to be ambushed. And what about you, do you automatically eavesdrop on what anybody says?"

"Of course," he said, before turning back to Jake. "After a while, Hale, you won't trust anybody. Except your partners, and your Echelon Leader of course. You have to trust them."

"Yeah, I guess," Lizzie said, suddenly looking out the window as the car turned up a winding tree-lined drive and through a high iron gate that closed automatically behind them. A great house began to come into view.

"Whoa," Jake said.

"Yeah, I'll second that," Lizzie said. "It looks like a castle, doesn't it?"

Filby glanced up from his screen and peered out the windshield. "No moat, no wall, no gate house, so technically it's not a castle. But... wow!"

"My house could fit inside it, three times over," Lizzie said.

"Stormglass headquarters probably could, too," Filby said.

"Except the missile silo," Lizzie said.

Filby hmmmed. "True. Good point."

Missile silo? Jake didn't ask. He was too busy gazing at the sprawling manor. He'd seen places this size before, but they were usually hospitals or libraries or university buildings. It was four stories high and made of stone, with countless arched windows, topped by peaked roofs, half a dozen chimneys, and a rounded tower at one end. To think that someone actually lived in this place — took showers here, watched TV, did laundry, ate meals — was almost unbelievable.

The car pulled up in the circular driveway, and the agents all climbed out. Two men emerged from the great doors of the manor to grab their backpacks, until Lizzie and Filby made it clear they'd all be carrying their own stuff, thanks. The servants melted away then, and a tall man in a suit — was he an actual butler? — waited for them in the doorway. Jake stared at him woozily, suddenly realizing how exhausted he was.

"Welcome to Mellifera Hall," he said, not quite looking at them. "I am Kaplan. You must be tired after your journey. The master thought you might like a few hours to sleep, so rooms have been prepared for you. Is that acceptable?"

"Sure thing, but looks like such a good day for a fox hunt," Lizzie said, squinting at the butler suspiciously.

"What a barbaric practice," the butler replied.

"That's the code," Filby whispered to Jake.

"Thanks," Lizzie said to the butler, "and tell your boss we said thanks. By the way…" She leant in to whisper to the man, but loud enough for Jake to hear. "Last time I ate breakfast in England, I got a big plate of blood sausage and smoked fish." She screwed up her face. "I don't know about that."

The butler didn't quite smile, but Jake thought it was a near thing. "Would bacon and eggs be more to your lady's liking?"

"My compliments to the chef, in advance," she said, stretching with a smile.

THE POISON GARDEN

Jake's room was like something out of an old movie: dark floral wallpaper, heavy velvet drapes, stone floors covered with thick patterned carpets, wooden dressers, and uncomfortable-looking upholstered chairs that were probably older than Jake's own house. The bed was as big as the YMCA swimming pool, with a tall wooden post at each corner, and a headboard and footboard carved with swoops and waves and curlicues. The bedspread weighed about a ton, and Jake didn't even try to climb underneath it, just kicked off his shoes and collapsed on top of the covers. He fell down into sleep almost immediately.

Some unknown time later, the door creaked, and Jake bolted up, then relaxed when he saw Lizzie at the door. "Breakfast time," she said. "I'd call it brunch, really, but I guess they don't do brunch here? Though they do tea at four o'clock in the afternoon, which is like bizarro opposite brunch, I guess. So get moving!"

Jake hurriedly showered and changed clothes, then wandered down the long hall until he found the big staircase that led to the grand entrance hall. From there he followed the sound of voices toward the dining room. He was a little disappointed it didn't have animal heads on the walls, but it was still majestic.

The table and chairs were heavy dark wood, and the sideboard along one wall was covered with rectangular metal dishes like an all-you-can-eat breakfast buffet. Filby had a plate of sliced fruit in front of him, and Lizzie was working her way through a pile of fluffy scrambled eggs almost as high as her head. Jake picked up a plate and scooped out sausage and eggs and bacon, passing over a few things he didn't recognize, or wished he didn't — like the tray of fried slices of tomato and whole smoked fish and some weird black discs that looked like black jello. Or was that the blood sausage Lizzie had talked about? *Ew.*

"We're meeting the entomologist after breakfast," Filby said. "He's waiting for us in his laboratory, so hurry up."

Jake obliged — the food was good, and there was heaps of it. He even experienced the rare and wonderful sensation of having enough bacon, which was usually impossible at his house, the way his dad sucked the stuff down. Soon they were all pushing back from the table, wiping their mouths on their cloth napkins. "We just leave the mess on the table?" Jake said.

"That's how it's done here," Lizzie said. "The dishes are someone else's problem. I wish it was like that at my house."

"You have to do dishes at home?" Filby asked, faking a gasp. "You should move!"

Lizzie rolled her eyes. "I like having my own room, thanks. I'm way too young to have a roommate!"

"And I'm safer if somebody drops a bomb on me," Filby said, leaning back and rubbing his belly.

Jake looked at them both quizzically. Was this the first time they'd started to talk about their home lives?

"So where do you guys live, anyway?" Jake asked.

"Sorry pal," Lizzie said mysteriously. "Your security clearance is way too low. Come on, let's go find this bee guy!"

Jake threw down his napkin and hurried after them. There'd be time to find out, later. They were working now, after all.

The three of them passed through hallways cluttered with shelves holding odd artifacts — bits of statues, cracked pots, carved elephant tusks, blue glass bottles — until they finally emerged into a sunny room at the back of the house, the walls and ceiling all panes of glass. Long tables held plants of every color, and it was moist and hot.

"Greenhouse," Lizzie said, leaning over to examine a purple flower. "Huh."

Filby leaned in. "This looks like monkshood," he said, before scanning the room more carefully. "That's bloodflower over there, and I see foxglove, lily of the valley, oleander, mountain laurel, yellow jessamine—"

"And now we know the Filster took a flower-arranging class at some point," Lizzie laughed.

Filby snorted. "So what's the name of this one, Lizzie?" She stood beside a plant almost her size, with purple bell-shaped flowers and dark attractive berries.

"Ummm…. Purple… berry… alia?"

He cleared his throat with an obviously fake cough, and blinked twice. "Atropa belladonna. Deadly nightshade. Eat three of these berries, and you're gone. And look over there!"

He pointed to an even taller plant with white flowers.

"That's hemlock," he said. "A couple seeds of that will kill you… This is a greenhouse full of poisonous flowers."

"Cool," cooed Lizzie.

"Don't touch them," Filby warned.

"Some of them, I would advise against even smelling." A man appeared at the end of a row of plants, removing a pair of dirt-stained gardening gloves. He was tall, thin, and old — older than Jake's granddad — with thinning wisps of gray hair around the bare, domelike top of his head.

"Hi," Filby said nervously. "We're looking for the Beekeeper."

"Aha, I see."

His eyes were bluish and mild, and he wore a suit much more worn and shabby than the butler's proper clothes. The cuffs of his jacket were brushed with soil.

"Are you the gardener?" Lizzie asked.

"I am," he agreed. "I also manage the apiary."

"The beehives," Filby said. "So you're the Beekeeper? This is your house?"

"The family estate, yes. It's terribly impractical, having such a big place for myself — half the rooms haven't been opened in years, not even to air them out — but I do enjoy the privacy." He looked down at them, head cocked, then nodded to himself. "So you three are Stormglass agents. It's hard to believe I was ever so young, but I suppose I must have been. Come along. We have a great deal to talk about."

"Wait a second," said Filby, without moving.

"Yes," said the Beekeeper.

"Where does your Queen live?"

The Beekeeper smiled then said, "Why, in a deck of fifty-two, of course."

"Okay, he's actually the Beekeeper."

"I thought you'd never ask. Now, I do hope one of you remembered to bring this curious bee, yes?"

Jake reached into his pocket, and carefully removed it. He held it out to the Beekeeper.

"And you must be the new agent?" he said, stooping down slightly to take the bundle. Jake nodded, and the Beekeeper smiled.

"Most interesting," he said as he unwrapped the cloth. "Most interesting, indeed. In fact, this could be the most brilliant thing I've ever seen!"

THE LABORATORY

Jake and Lizzie and Filby rushed to keep up with the Beekeeper as he raced back down the corridors.

"Have you heard of colony collapse disorder," he asked without looking back.

"No," they all said.

"Honeybees all across the globe are disappearing, and dying. It's a terrible thing, and not a soul knows the reason. It began slowly, before any of you were born, so slowly that none of us really took notice. But by the time the three of you," he looked back and did a quick calculation in his head, "yes, by the time the three of you were born, almost all the wild honeybees in your America were already gone." He shook his head, keeping his rapid pace through the halls and taking another right.

"Bees aren't gone," insisted Jake, struggling to keep up. "I see them all the time."

"Honeybees, my boy. But it gets worse. Not so long ago, they began to die in captivity as well."

"So what causes it?" Jake asked. *How does this old man move so fast?*

"Yes, that is the question. So much money and determination and time has gone into trying to find an explanation of what's happening, but there is none! Could it be a pesticide?" He glanced back at

Jake, who shrugged his shoulders. "No, no, no, it's probably not a pesticide. Perhaps it's changing temperatures? Yes, it could be. It could be an infection, or mites, perhaps a fungus... But so many of us beekeepers have lost our hives already." He stopped suddenly and swerved about.

"So, young agents, how does this relate to your bee?"

He reached out and grabbed the nearest door handle. "Ah, the laboratory," he said, thrusting open the door.

Unlike the rest of the house, this laboratory was of the future. Jake stared glassy-eyed at the digital flat screens mounted to each wall. Images of molecules floated on some, while others showed rotating DNA strands. A trio of screens played what appeared to be live security camera footage of a busy sidewalk in a city somewhere. Was that London? One huge screen featured a life-size x-ray of a human body, with a bullet's path digitally drawn through it. Medical terms and data scrolled past. A wall of shelves was covered with curious bottles, each marked by small digital labels, and a glistening metal coil rested on a pedestal — and emitted popping sparks of electricity. In the middle of it all sat a very cluttered wooden desk, covered in papers and cables and tweezers and scalpels and junk.

"Welcome to my crime lab," said the Beekeeper as he swept aside a clearing on the desk and sat down behind it. "I'm not a technology expert by any means, but I do like to try and keep up."

"This is amazing," said Lizzie, looking around.

"Yeah," Filby agreed, eyes wide. "It reminds me of Iron Lynx's lab."

The Beekeeper smiled. "You know young Lynx, eh? I guess he's not so young anymore, but he was once a student of mine. And my, look how the tables have turned. I'm struggling to keep up with technology, while he set up all of this." He swept out an arm, waving at the walls and the screens. "Now, does anyone happen to have a HyperOpticon at hand? I seem to have misplaced mine again..."

While Filby reached into his satchel, Jake stared at the wall of bottles. One contained a spent cartridge floating in amber liquid, and the label read "Case 987-412B Assassination Attempt. Click for more information." He lightly touched the label, which beeped briefly then rearranged itself to read, "Requires Higher Security Clearance." He sighed and turned away. He really needed to get better security clearance.

The Beekeeper yanked a pair of goggles from a drawer and pulled them over his almost-bald head.

"Hold the HyperOpticon right here," he said. "Actually, plug it in first. That would be helpful. Yes, right over there."

As soon as Filby plugged his gadget into the cable, every flat screen switched to a shaky close-up of the bee on the table. The Vindiqo logo appeared bright and huge, and the Beekeeper leaned in with a small pair of tweezers.

"Ah, the logo. A nice touch. Yes, oversized fore and hind wings," he muttered. "Interesting. Faster travel for the modern age, longer distances. Incredible pollen baskets, improved pollen press… fascinating. Oh, the rakes are absolutely beautiful. What delicate work, a master! Can you move the HyperOpticon over a little, yes — right there! Look at the mandibles. Those are sharp. Could do quite a bit of damage. Interesting antennae… huge, really. Would help with improving communications skills between the bees. Hm. A good way to make contact with others? But look at this stinger. Now that's really quite odd."

He pressed the tweezers to the stinger lightly, and it barely bent. He pressed it harder, and again it barely gave at all. "Could that make sense?" he asked himself, then picked up what looked like a pen and triggered a switch on the side. A thin laser beam shot out.

"Now do keep the HyperOpticon steady if you can, agent. This is delicate work."

As the Beekeeper carefully sliced through the bee with the laser, Filby turned a shade of green and Lizzie moved closer. "This is cool," she said, watching the skin part ways. Jake saw miniature bee guts magnified in high resolution across three walls.

"Well, it's most clearly real," said the Beekeeper, separating the bee's insides with the tweezers. He seemed utterly lost in his thoughts.

"Ah, what a proboscis. Longer, stronger, almost perfect. The bee will certainly be able to feed itself. Standard digestive system, perhaps a little improved.

And a venom sac, as expected, but..." He paused, and looked up at the three children for a second before looking down again. "Why would it be like this? That makes no sense at all. The venom sac is so much bigger, and so much thicker... stronger..."

He pulled and stretched at the membrane, and his words drifted off as he set the tweezers down slowly, and adjusted his body until he sat upright again. He gazed at the door, lost in thought. No one spoke, and Jake waited for one beat, and then two, and then a third, before asking his question.

"What happened?"

The Beekeeper shook himself out of his reverie, and looked at Jake with a nervous smile. "Well, the good news is," he said, "this bee might just save us from the end of the world."

VIPERBEES

They went outside, into the cool shade of a great tree, and sat around a wrought-iron table where a sweating pitcher of lemonade waited, along with several glasses. The Beekeeper poured them each a glass, then sat down, crossed one leg over another, and gazed out across the back lawn of his estate. Jake looked, too, at the gentle hills and distant trees, and at the peculiar arrangement of white boxes off in the distance — they looked a bit like a bunch of filing cabinets, but why would filing cabinets be sitting out in a field?

"What do you know about bees?" the Beekeeper looked to Jake, and said at last.

Jake cleared his throat.

"What everybody knows, I guess. They make honey. They live in hives. They sting you if they get angry or scared. They pollinate flowers and fruit trees and stuff, so we need bees for those things to grow. Right?"

"Precisely," the Beekeeper said. "Eloquently phrased, and absolutely accurate. They pollinate flowers and fruit trees, and stuff. Let's focus on the stuff. You may not realize how important bees are. An old friend of mine, a Stormglass scientist I worked with many years ago, hypothesized that if the bee disappeared, we would have no more than four years to live. Mankind would become extinct."

Jake blinked. Four years? He wouldn't even be done with school in four years.

The beekeeper calmly sipped his lemonade and went on. "Yes, we would start by losing all that delicious honey, which would be a pity indeed. But we'd forget about honey quickly. We'd lose all the crops that are fertilized by honeybees, as well. More than just the flowers in your garden and the peach trees, we'd lose the stuff. In your country, that means several hundred thousand different types of plants. They'd all be gone. Evaporated. Dead. Tell me, agent, do you like fast food?"

"Sure," Jake said, confused.

"Excellent. That will still exist without bees — McDonald's, VindiBurger, and so on. You'll be eating a lot of it at first. Processed foods, as well. But most fruit and vegetables will be gone, forever. But that's just the beginning, the small change. If the bees are gone" He started to count on his fingers. "First the food chain collapses, which means animals will start to starve. That would be crippling. Then the predators that fed on those animals — and of course I include us — well, we'll start to die too. No fruit, no vegetables, no meat. It's extremely unfortunate, but with the loss of bees, the death would keep coming."

The Beekeeper took out a pocket watch and studied it for a second, as if calculating the time they had left. "Without bees," he said to the watch, "we'd be faced with mass global extinction."

The three agents stared at him, aghast.

"But what does all this have to do with the bee we found?" asked Lizzie.

"Ah," the Beekeeper said. "This is where it gets interesting. There are about twenty thousand different types of bee. I haven't seen them all, I won't see them all, but I can say with absolute certainty that — as you've probably already guessed — your bee isn't one of them. It's entirely new. The logo on the bottom clearly points to it as coming from a company called Vindiqo Products and Research."

"You guys were right," said Jake, eyes wide. "But why does the bee even have a logo on it?"

"My initial hypothesis," he said, "is that you've stumbled on a new Vindiqo product. It appears that through genetic wizardry and some remarkable crossbreeding, they've managed to develop a new honeybee to replace those that are dying, a honeybee that could save the planet! This bee is larger and stronger than any breed I've seen. It could travel further distances at greater speeds, could pollinate more plants, and could actually prevent global catastrophe!"

"So... this is a good thing?" Jake said hesitantly. Something in the Beekeeper's voice didn't convince him it was, and the Beekeeper didn't respond immediately. Instead, he studied his glass of lemonade and tapped his fingers on the side of his chair for several drawn-out seconds.

"There's just something off," he said. "Something not quite right. All the productive elements of the bee

— the pollen handlers, various useful bits and bobs — are so wonderfully improved. But so are other... less productive elements."

"What do you mean?"

The Beekeeper moved to the edge of his seat, and leaned in to the young agents.

"The stinger is stronger than it needs to be, far stronger — something like a steel — and it's not barbed like a traditional honeybee's stinger. It's straight, which means this bee could hypothetically sting someone without dying. Could sting someone many, many times in fact."

"Wow," said Lizzie. "I thought that was the saving grace of the bee, that it could only sting you once..."

"Precisely. And the mandibles — they're a pair of pliers bees use for various tasks — on this bee, they're sharp and jagged like a bread knife, which is completely unnecessary. I just don't see any reason for that."

The beekeeper paused, considering whether to continue. He looked at the three agents, and leaned forward even further. His voice was low.

"What worries me the most, though—"

And then the Beekeeper jumped. He looked around confused, reached down in his pocket, and plucked out his vibrating mobile phone.

"Ah, it's Cyrus Rex," he said reading a text message. "He wants the three of you back at Stormglass headquarters, post haste."

"Cyrus who?" Jake asked.

"His is the hand that guides us," the Beekeeper said, putting his phone away and standing up. "He's the president of Stormglass, the Colonel. It will take a few hours to arrange the flight. In the meantime, would you like to see my hives? They're quite safe, and if you're going to be dealing with bees on this mission, it might be useful for you to spend time with a few."

"But what about what were you about to say? Something worries you," Jake said.

"Oh, no, no. I'm quite sure it's nothing to worry about. I must be mistaken. Let's see the bees."

"Do we get to dress up in those big beekeeper suits?" Lizzie said.

The Beekeeper laughed. "Is anyone allergic to bee stings?"

All three shook their heads no.

"Well, then I think veils should be sufficient. Bees attempting to defend their hives are attracted by your breath, and — I will say from experience — being stung on the face isn't pleasant. Do as I say, and you should be fine. I'll bring a smoker just in case."

"What's that?" asked Jake.

"Oh, just a beekeeping tool. The smoke calms the bees down, and fools them into thinking there's a forest fire. They dive into their hives to eat as much honey as they can, and we, meanwhile, avoid getting stung."

After asking the butler Kaplan to arrange the flight, he led them to a wooden shed and outfitted them with white hoods, each with a square mesh screen in front of the face, so they could see out. The hood was hot, completely blocked Jake's peripheral vision, and didn't seem like the ideal thing for a spy to wear... but if they weren't safe on some ex-secret-agent's country estate, they weren't safe anywhere.

The Beekeeper led them toward the white filing cabinets, which turned out to be wooden hives made of stacked boxes, eighteen of them scattered across a large area of the lawn. Bees zoomed out and returned to the hives steadily, with some hovering around the entry points on guard duty. These bees were much smaller and more dull-looking than the manufactured bee — and a lot less cartoonish. The Beekeeper lifted his smoker and sprayed a sweet-smelling cloud around one of the hives. The buzzing bees slowed down, crawling back into the hive. "Would anyone like a spot of fresh honey?" he asked. "There's absolutely nothing like it."

A distant whump-whump-whump and a movement in the sky caught Jake's attention, and he squinted. "Is that a helicopter?"

"Hmm," the Beekeeper said, looking up. "Not so many of those around here—"

The helicopter was small, black, and very fast, starting as a dot at the far end of the grounds but rapidly growing larger as it approached.

"Perhaps Stormglass sent a helicopter to give us a ride?" Filby said.

"A transatlantic helicopter ride?" Lizzie said. "I don't think so."

"Agents," the Beekeeper said, his voice tight, "I think we should get back to the greenhouse. Quickly!"

BEE BOMBS

Lizzie and Filby instantly began sprinting for the house, and the Beekeeper went after them with even greater speed than Jake could have expected. Jake wasn't as quick — see, that's why he needed training! — but he caught up to them fast enough. The helicopter's rotors were incredibly loud now, and when Jake glanced over his shoulder he saw it hovering over the Beekeeper's hives. A door slid open on the side of the helicopter, and there were people inside, dressed in full white beekeeper suits. They were throwing something out of the helicopter, lots of small boxes —

Jake stumbled on a divot in the grass and turned his attention back to running. He reached the greenhouse just after the others, and the Beekeeper slammed the door after him, and watched the helicopter grimly. He pulled out his cellphone, pressed a single button, and spoke quickly.

"Kaplan, the estate is under attack."

"Attack?" Jake said as the helicopter tipped slightly, swung its nose around, and flew toward the greenhouse. It passed overhead, and all of them craned their heads to watch it through the glass ceiling. Another box fell from the helicopter, this one crashing into the greenhouse's roof, but not breaking it. The box split and scores of small buzzing shapes spilled out, crawling on the glass and flying into the garden. Then the helicopter rose rapidly and flew away, the sound of its rotors fading quickly.

"Bees," the Beekeeper said. To Jake's surprise, he climbed up on a table and peered up, trying to get a closer look. "They're big, like the one you brought." He peered closer. "Yes, they're surely from Vindiqo."

"If that glass breaks..." Filby said nervously.

The Beekeeper shook his head. "It's reinforced. I was an agent long enough to know caution is always necessary. Don't worry. We'll get this... sorted out." He climbed back down from the table, and held his hand to his head as he watched his hives. A swarm of the Vindiqo bees had surrounded one of the hives. They were attacking the Beekeeper's own bees.

"I think now is probably the right time to express my concerns," said the Beekeeper, staring out as more Vindiqo bees collected on the windows.

All three agents turned to him.

"The venom sac was larger and far stronger than it should have been."

"What's the venom sac?" asked Jake.

"Perhaps you've been stung by a bee before. The venom sac is where the bee carries its poison. Normally, the poison isn't very toxic — it doesn't really harm most humans. But in this bee you brought, this miracle bee if you will... not only was the stinger so much stronger, but the venom sac was like none I'd seen before. It was reinforced, as if the bee was made to carry something more... poisonous."

"A biological weapon," said Filby, as the buzzing sound around them grew louder.

"I think you mean a *bee*-ological weapon," Lizzie joked, then turned bright red as she realized how inappropriate it was.

The Beekeeper looked at her, eyes wide, and then let out a loud laugh. "I say, that's really very good... a bee-ological weapon! I must remember that... But—" He turned distractedly into a closet and started pulling out metal canisters and rods.

"It's a nice theory," Filby said. "Except for the part where it doesn't make any sense."

Lizzie scowled at him. "What are you talking about? It's totally the sort of thing Vindiqo would do—"

Jake shook his head. "No, Filby's right." Lizzie turned her glare on him, and he held up his hands. "I'm sorry, but he is. The logo, Lizzie. If you were making a deadly poisonous murder-bee, why would you put your company logo on its belly? That's just crazy."

"Okay," she said. "I guess that is one point."

"No, no, they're right," the Beekeeper said, pulling several bee suits from a cabinet. "Vindiqo is a huge, successful corporation. They wouldn't use the bees for such evil purposes. But they have connections to the underworld, who wouldn't have such qualms! They'd probably start by testing them on animals, of course."

"So that's why the cats were all dead," said Jake.

"Dead cats?" the Beekeeper said, dropping a heavy box onto a table and swerving around. "What?"

"Didn't they tell you," said Lizzie, shocked. "Wasn't it in your mission briefing? I thought you knew. We found the bee where a dozen dead cats were found. They were swollen and blistered and covered in puncture marks."

"Oh," whispered the Beekeeper. "Swollen and blistered? That would make it a deadly poison. Well, at least that explains another small mystery."

"What's that?"

"These bees outside don't have Vindiqo's logo on their bellies. It seems these bees were sent here for another purpose. I'd suppose these bees were sent to silence us."

"What do we do?" Lizzie said.

"We do what we must," the Beekeeper said, watching the bees swarm around the greenhouse and his hives. He suddenly looked much older and more tired than he had before, but a fire raged in his eyes. "Suit up, agents. We'll kill them with fire."

They all stood together at the greenhouse door, each armored in a full beekeeper's suit. Jake and Filby wore tanks of pesticide strapped to their backs, and held sprayer rods in their gloved hands.

"Be careful with this," Kaplan said as he strapped a flamethrower tank onto Lizzie's back. "Please be very careful." Kaplan then picked up a second flamethrower, and threw it onto his own back. Kaplan had hung netting around the door, and all five crowded inside it, close to the door.

"Get your squirt gun out of my mask," said Lizzie to Filby.

"Keep your flamethrower out of mine," said Filby.

"Agents," said the Beekeeper. "Is everybody ready?"

Jake noticed that while the Beekeeper was also dressed in a beekeeper suit, he was only armed with a spray can of lemon-scented furniture polish and a net.

"Are you sure that's enough," Jake asked.

"Bees adore this polish," said the Beekeeper, taking the door handle and throwing it open. "Now!" he cried.

Everyone ran outside, and almost immediately the air reeked of chemicals and smoke. Jake sprayed left and right, trying to hit the thickest clouds of bees, and taking care not to hit Lizzie as she ran by. A column of flames exploded from the end of her pipe, nearly knocking her off balance. "Watch out," Filby screamed as a line of fire came dangerously close to his body.

Kaplan the butler held a can of gasoline — he called it "petrol" — in the one hand and a rag in the other. After splashing the gas around the hives, he tied the bit of cloth around a stick, lit the cloth with a lighter, and tossed the flaming stick at the hives from a safe distance.

The gas caught with a *whump*, and the fire soon spread to the other hives, all flickering red and yellow. He took the flamethrower tube into his hands, and sprayed flames into the swarm. Bees tried to flee the hive, but the smoke seemed to disorient them, and they fell from the air.

As if in a calmer universe, the Beekeeper misted the air with his lemon-scented spray. With an urgent flick of his wrist, he whipped his net around. "Caught you," he'd yell, as he captured another live bee.

Jake and Filby drenched the outside of the greenhouse, spraying it with whooshing shots of liquid poison. Vindiqo bees and real bees fell to the ground squirming. Jake didn't have time to feel guilty. Instead, he sweated inside the baking hot suit and worried about what would happen if even one bee managed to find a way in. It would probably sting him to death.

"Over here," shouted Lizzie. She stood away from everyone else, spraying a line of fire. "I need help," she cried.

Jake looked around, but no one else heard her. He wondered why her suit wasn't white, and suddenly realized it wasn't only the air that was thick with fake bees — she was crawling with them! They'd covered her!

"Help me," she cried. Jake ran to her, but didn't know what to do. He started slapping at her back with his gloved hands. It made no difference — the bees would merely fly to a different part of her body.

"Don't just stand there," she cried as more bugs landed. "Spray me, Hale!"

Jake yelled out and stepped backwards. "Shut your eyes," he cried.

He shut his own eyes, too, and pulled the trigger hard, drenching her in a spray of poison. "Don't breathe," he yelled as he opened his eyes again and aimed for her mask. Bees slipped from her suit, collapsing to the ground in the thick spray. Jake kept shooting, and shooting, and shooting until her suit was drenched and white.

Eventually, it was over. The air was still, and the grass covered with the corpses of thousands of dead bees.

"There could be more," the Beekeeper said, then looked back at his own hives. "But mine are gone."

Jake patted the Beekeeper awkwardly on the back. "You can get more bees, right?"

"I suppose," he said, voice muffled. "But these were the fabric of my family. They were my own father's bees. The honey from these bees has been on my table since I was a child, and no honey will ever taste the same. And now that family legacy is just..." He gestured at the smoke and blackened patches of grass and was unable to speak for a few seconds. Then he stood up straight.

"As you progress with this investigation, agents, do me one favor."

"Yeah?" Lizzie said.

"They're only bees," the Beekeeper said. "Just insects. But that makes no difference... avenge them."

The same silent driver transported the three of them away from the great house, but not to the same airfield as before — they drove two hours to a landing strip even smaller and more deserted-looking. They took with them a small tub of dead bees, for analysis at headquarters. The Beekeeper was working on a special container for the live bees, and would ship them separately. No one wanted to risk those killers getting loose into nature.

The jet waiting for them looked exactly the same as the one that had flown them to England, though the numbers written on the tail were different. Inside it appeared identical, which made Jake think the tail numbers had been altered to cover their tracks. The spy business sure was complicated.

This time Filby didn't get immediately absorbed in his Stormpad, but sat on the couch staring into space, frowning and chewing on his lower lip. "What is going on," he asked out loud.

Jake slid into a chair across from Lizzie at a little table, and she brought out a deck of cards and with a devilish smile suggested they play War.

"I feel like I've been in a war," Jake said exhaustedly as Lizzie dealt out the deck. They all still reeked of smoke and gasoline and pesticide, since there hadn't been time to shower.

"It's not the first time somebody dropped something on me from a helicopter," Lizzie said, laying down some cards. "But it's the first time anybody's ever dropped killer bees on me. I wouldn't mind if it's the last."

Jake turned over his next card. "So what's headquarters like?"

"I'm not gonna tell you," she said with a taunting smile. "Your security clearance is way too low. They'll have to do something about that before they even open the door for you. Plus, I don't want to spoil the surprise!"

"Okay, then — can you tell me where it is?" He played a nine of clubs.

She shook her head. "I don't even know that! I've tried to work it out, but they jam the GPS when you get close, they don't fly by any landmarks, and if you come by car, they actually black out the windows! All I know is it's the middle of nowhere." She laid a nine of diamonds on top of Jake's nine of clubs, and grinned. "I'm sure you realize this means war?"

AUTONOMOUS

After flying for hours and sleeping as much as they could, they landed in a rocky desert: a great expanse of nothing, broken up by heaps of boulders, with distant hills covered by ugly, scratchy bushes. "Home sweet home," Filby said with a fond smile, resting on the couch beside Jake.

"What do you mean?" Jake asked.

Filby squinted, and then said, "I live here."

"You live at Stormglass? What about your family?"

"Stormglass is my family," he said with an eager smile.

"But your parents?"

Filby shook his head. "You know, it's like boarding school."

"I couldn't stand living here," Lizzie said, leaning in. "You can't sneak out at night without triggering a dozen alarms."

Jake peered out the windows. There wasn't even an airfield — just emptiness, dotted by occasional rocks, without a single building in sight.

Filby grinned. "But wait until you see the library. It's huge!" He glanced at his Stormpad. "We're early."

They climbed out into the rocky terrain, and the pilot barely paused before taxiing and taking off again. Lizzie dropped her bag in the dirt and sat on it.

Filby shaded his eyes and scanned the horizon, then pointed. "There, Hale, see the dust?"

Jake squinted, then nodded. Something was coming their way from the west, where the sun was sinking toward the horizon. They waited, and in a few minutes, a low-slung, dusty red vehicle that looked like a cross between a dune buggy and an SUV slowed to a stop in front of them. The machine was bright red... but there was no driver.

"Um," Jake said, "is this, like, remote controlled or something? Like a Mars rover?"

"It's an autonomous vehicle," Filby said.

Lizzie patted the machine's hood, and said, "Her name is Hermes. She's self-driving. She was designed for the DARPA Grand Challenge, but then the inventors gave her to Stormglass instead."

"The DARPA what?" Jake walked around the car and peered into the lenses of the cameras protruding from the grille.

"You don't know the Grand Challenge?" Lizzie said. "It's a big race that's only for vehicles — no drivers are allowed!"

"No drivers?"

"None at all. Picture it: dozens of empty cars, racing across the desert. It's amazing."

"So what's DARPA?"

"The Defense Advanced Research Projects Agency," said Filby with authority, as he climbed into Hermes. "They do research on artificial intelligence, flying cars, body armor, robots..."

"Get in, Hale," said Lizzie. "Now we're riding in style!"

Jake fumbled to strap himself into the complicated set of buckles and seatbelts. "Is this even safe?"

"Hold on tight, Hale," Lizzie said. "It's not a smooth ride."

Hermes's engine roared, and the vehicle surged forward, the sudden acceleration pressing Jake hard against the seat. The desert outside the dusty windows blurred, and when the car hit a bump, they flew in the air and slammed back down with a hard bounce that made Lizzie whoop with excitement. She grabbed a microphone and shouted through it, her voice booming across the desert from speakers hidden in the front grille. Jake tried to relax, to imagine that he was on an amusement park ride, but a car driving itself was just too weird.

Then again, they were all way too young to drive, so it kind of made sense.

After about ten minutes of high-speed bumps, jumps, yells and jostling, Hermes decelerated and came to a stop... next to a heap of boulders about the size of Jake's garage.

They climbed out of the car, and Jake reached out to stretch his aching limbs. Hermes raced off into the desert, leaving them in a cloud of dust that gradually blew away. The sun wasn't quite down, but it was getting close, and the temperature was dropping. It was going to be a cold night in the desert.

"What now?" Jake said. "A giant mech-suit comes and picks us up and carries us the rest of the way?"

"There's no rest of the way, new kid," Lizzie said. "We're here."

Filby thumped one of the boulders, saying "Any minute now...", and then it opened. Jake laughed because it was so unexpected: a curved bit of rock swinging out just like an ordinary door.

Inside the boulder, gleaming metal doors slid apart to reveal a sleek glossy elevator with black bubble surveillance cameras mounted on the ceiling. Filby stepped inside and placed his hand on a black glass panel, which pulsed blue. Lizzie followed him and did the same. Jake went in after them, glanced at Lizzie for confirmation, then placed his hand on the screen.

It pulsed red, and Lizzie gasped, but then a soothing voice spoke from a speaker near the ceiling. "Temporary level three security clearance granted," it said, and the red glow turned blue.

Filby leaned against the wall and swallowed. "That's good. I'd hate to think what would happen if someone unauthorized tried to use this elevator. I'm sure it would take them somewhere, but it wouldn't be anywhere you'd want to go. Security is serious here — it's even protected against an EMP being set off outside the building! There's nowhere safer than Stormglass."

There were no buttons to press for different floors, but instead the elevator just began to descend. There was no indication of where they were headed or how long it would even take to get there. It was certainly the longest elevator ride Jake had ever taken, and with every passing minute he got more excited.

Finally, the elevator slowed and stopped. The doors slid open, and Jake followed his friends into the gleaming heart of Stormglass.

WELCOME TO STORMGLASS

The first thing Jake noticed was the vastness: Stormglass Headquarters filled a cavern so large it could have held Angleton Park with room to spare. It was illuminated by spheres of white light suspended from wires dangling down from the impossibly high ceiling. The air was cool, but not cold, and Jake struggled to take in the scene.

Offices and corridors had been cut into the stone walls on all sides — levels and levels of them, all behind walls of glass that were sometimes transparent and sometimes dark. A waterfall rushed down a cavern wall far to the left, plunging from the darkness above and disappearing into darkness below, and providing a background rumble of constant white noise. A few agents practiced rock-climbing along bare patches of the cavern walls — they looked like they were Jake's age, or maybe a little older — and two other agents were rappelling down ropes from the ceiling. Everywhere Jake looked, there were tunnels disappearing deeper into the earth, and Jake wondered how big this place really was.

The floor beneath their feet was a shining expanse of polished black marble flecked with small white glittering stones, and there was a giant golden "S" in the stone. There were people walking around the space, or riding Segway-style personal scooters, or riding in golf carts — dozens of people, at least, all hurrying purposefully around — but still the place seemed almost deserted, so great was its size.

"This place is crazy," Jake said, awestruck.

"It can be a lot to take in," Filby said with a small, proud smile. "It started as a missile base, but now we live here. Security is so tight that even I've only seen a few of the levels."

A young woman strode purposefully toward them, dressed in a white t-shirt and gray sweatpants, her blonde ponytail swinging side to side as she walked, a big welcoming grin and a pair of horn-rimmed glasses on her face. Filby waved and Lizzie ran to her and gave her a hug.

Filby said, "That's our Echelon Leader, Jenny. She's great."

Jenny reminded Jake instantly of a babysitter he'd had one year, a teenager who worked summers as a camp counselor and always had ideas for a million projects. Jake guessed she was maybe eighteen or nineteen years old.

"You must be Hale," she exclaimed, holding out her hand as Jake realized he'd heard her on his Stormpad. "Great to have you on the team. I've been reading Filby and Lizzie's reports, and your work so far is wonderful. I'm your Echelon Leader, Gold Eagle – but feel free to call me Jenny."

She leaned in to whisper, "That's not my real name, either."

Lizzie and Filby both grabbed Jake. "We're in the same echelon," shouted Lizzie.

"That's fantastic," shouted Filby.

"Sure—" Jake began, "But what's an echelon?"

Jenny had already swiveled toward Filby and Lizzie with a broad smile. "Enough cheering already. You two have a debriefing with Snakesman, two minutes ago."

Both Lizzie and Filby cheered.

"You two get moving. He's up on level three, in the Stratus Room."

"See you later, Hale." Lizzie reached over to give his hand a squeeze. "Don't worry, you'll do great."

She and Filby set off across the floor toward one of the tunnels near the waterfall, and Jake turned back to Jenny, suddenly feeling very alone and overwhelmed. "So... what happens to me now?"

"First I'll take you to your quarters, so you can put down your bag, then you should probably call your parents and let them know you're doing okay, and then... it's time for orientation!"

Jake's mom and dad were thrilled he was having a good time, and he didn't even bother telling them about the Beekeeper and Stormglass HQ; he didn't lie, but he didn't volunteer it, because they wouldn't believe him anyway. After he made the call and gave the phone back to Jenny, she tapped her watch. "Time to get started. Walk with me. No, leave your bag there." She set off down the hallway, long legs taking big steps, and Jake hurried to keep up. The hallway was tiled in alternating squares of white and black, and lit by recessed LED lights, and they passed dozens of closed, unmarked doors, many with handprint readers embedded in the walls next to them. Jenny took numerous turnings down countless identical corridors, choosing directions seemingly at random.

"Normally," Jenny said, "we bring in new agents for at least two weeks of spy training." She waved hello to an older kid in the hallway, wearing a flak jacket and a badge.

"Someone's seen Kim Kyok-un," the kid whispered as he passed. "A bunch of us are being sent out."

"Good luck," said Jenny, before turning back to Jake. "Kim's one of the real bad guys. Where was I? Ah, yes, normally we'd teach you disguise, evasion, unarmed combat, but we don't have time for that. We need you back in the field, immediately. This bee business is serious."

"So I don't get training?" Jake tried to keep the disappointment out of his voice.

"Oh, you'll get training later, but in the meantime you get accelerated training. This will be your crash-course in spycraft, focusing only on skills you're likely to need on this mission — observation, escape, a little combat, interrogation, and whatever else we can cram into you. Sound fun?"

"It does, actually," Jake said with a wide smile.

"Oh, good." She suddenly stopped, spun on her heel and looked down at him, arms crossed. "Then here's your first test: we've been walking down these corridors for three minutes. Where's the room with your bag?"

Jake was annoyed for a second, and then laughed. "I should have known you'd be testing me." He turned around and looked down the corridor, thinking back over the route they'd taken. He'd always had a good sense of direction — he never had any problem finding his way out of the corn maze at the harvest festival, and he'd impressed his mom by leading them out of a house of mirrors last summer. "This way," he said, with more confidence than he felt, and started walking.

The corridors weren't quite identical. Some stretches of hallway had handprint scanners on every door, and some stretches only had one or two. He hadn't exactly memorized the way, but when he looked down some corridors they just felt wrong. So he trusted his instincts, and as the two continued walking, he felt more and more confident. After five minutes he stopped before a door, and placed his hand to the panel. It beeped, sprang open, and there was his bag sitting in the middle of the bed.

"Not bad," Jenny said with an impressed smile. "Not bad at all. I'd heard you were observant. And you can do card tricks, right? If so, you can pick locks. We'll work on sharpening those skills for now. Sound good?"

"Sounds good." *As long as I learn to jump out of airplanes at some point*, he thought.

Jenny grinned. "So tell me — do you feel like exercising your body right now, or your mind?"

"My mind, I guess," he said. "I'm a little tired from all the traveling."

"Body it is," Jenny said brightly, and patted him on the shoulder. "Sorry, Hale. This will be good practice for you. And if the training becomes too hard, just say the word and we'll stop."

Jake narrowed his eyes. "And what happens if I ask you to stop?"

"We'll drop you off at home, and you'll never hear from us again."

"That's kind of what I figured," he said.

"Come on — it's time to sweat."

THE TRAITOR (2)

The traitor hid in the last stall of an otherwise-empty Stormglass bathroom and spoke in barely a whisper. "Did you have to drop the bees?"

"Oh, my goodness, what a horrible accident that was," the Doctor said convincingly. "So utterly regrettable! The bees weren't even supposed to be in the helicopter — the operatives were only scheduled to drop a listening device. A bug, not the bugs, I'd ordered... But I was so glad to hear no one was injured. I wouldn't have been able to forgive myself otherwise." He coughed, and the cough sounded for just a second like a swallowed laugh.

"The fire almost..." the traitor started.

"You would never have been harmed, my young friend. You're too resourceful, brave, and amazing. And the others are smart enough that they were able to handle the situation. Who knows, perhaps this will even work to our advantage. Old Cyrus Rex will have no choice but to devote time and resources to the bees, now!"

"I guess... but aren't you worried about exposing me? There was no way Vindiqo could have known about the trip to the estate, if I hadn't told you—"

"Nonsense," the Doctor said brusquely, but then caught himself and his voice turned into thick treacle.

"That's not something you need to worry about. Rex doesn't have any idea about the true extent of our surveillance network, and — to let you in on a very secretive secret — nor do you! So many Stormglass agents have become dissatisfied, you're not the only one. And on our payroll we have pilots, drivers, perhaps even a butler on the Beekeeper's staff – so there's no reason they would ever suspect you."

"Are you sure?"

"So sure, my friend. So absolutely sure. Now stick to your assignment, act loyal to these agents of good, and remember — only Mundt knows you're working for us, so our soldiers will certainly be working against you. So be careful, yes? But you're doing perfectly. And don't forget about the files... they're so terribly important."

"I'm taking care of them now," the traitor said.

"Excellent," the Doctor said. "With our efforts from the outside, and yours from the inside, there is no way we can fail my friend."

CRASH COURSE

The next morning, Jake stumbled through the cafeteria line, his muscles aching, and his brain swimming with facts and thoughts. He couldn't decide if he was more hungry or exhausted.

Lizzie slid into line beside him and nudged him in the ribs. Jake almost fell over.

"Wow... I'm wiped out."

"I spent the afternoon working with Dantes," Lizzie said, excited, "Did you have him?"

Jake shook his head.

"He's hilarious — a total master of disguise! Even after you've met him a dozen times, he can still fool you. He changes his voice, the way he stands, the way he moves, everything."

"It would be nice to be with someone so relaxing," Jake said wistfully.

"So what exactly did you do yesterday?" Lizzie started heaping her plate with scrambled eggs.

"I met Iron Tiger first."

Lizzie grinned. "Freerunning! So now you're sliding down railings and leaping fences and somersaulting off roofs?"

"I guess," Jake said. They moved to a table, where Filby was already demolishing a heap of French toast. "Right now, though, I can barely walk," Jake continued, sitting down across from Filby. "All those catwalks and trash cans and fences and walls to climb up and jump over, that was insane. But then I had Master D."

"Self-defense!" Lizzie cried, and aimed a punch at Filby's shoulder. He lifted a hand without even looking at her, turning her blow so deftly that she cracked her knuckles on the table.

"Ouch," she cried, as Filby caught Jake's eye and smirked. "When did you get so much better at self-defense?"

"Just practice, I guess," said Filby, looking proud of himself. "And I'm on a diet, so you better watch out." He rubbed his hands together and laughed.

"You know Master D was an agent just a few years ago, right?" said Lizzie. "All of the teachers were."

"Even I was," Jenny said, sitting down with a smile. "You've got an appointment, Agent Hale. Ten, nine, eight, seven," and Jake finished off his glass of milk and got to his feet before she hit zero.

"Try not to break him Jenny, okay," Filby called. "We're going to need him!"

"Today we're working out his brain," Jenny said. "Mostly." As they left the cafeteria, she added, "You're meeting Snakesman."

Jenny led him down a glistening tunnel filled with security cameras that ended at an unmarked steel door. "Here's where I leave you," Jenny said.

The door had no handle, no knob, nothing at all.

"Uh... what am I supposed to do?"

"Go through the door and see Snakesman," she said. "Shoo!" She turned and walked away.

Jake scanned the wall, and saw a brick that looked a bit different from the others, just a bit lighter in color. Thinking of the loose brick from the failed dead drop, he pulled on it, and it revealed a ten-digit keypad.

"Hey!" Jake called to Jenny's back, "What's the combination?"

"Good luck!" Jenny called, her laugh floating back from far down the corridor.

LOCKS AND LIES

Jake grinned. Fine. He was good at tests. He peered at the keypad. The buttons were rubber, and most of them were pretty worn out. The worn buttons were probably used in the combination, since they had clearly been pushed the most often. Still, there had to be a better way, something more conclusive...

He opened up his backpack and considered. He had an ultraviolet flashlight, and a little bottle of fluorescent fluid for finding fingerprints and blood. He gently spritzed the mist on the keypad and then switched on the special light.

A few of the keys glowed with faint smudges under the light, showing the smears of oily fingertips: numbers 2, 3, 4, 5, 6 and 8. He groaned. Six digits! Even assuming each digit was only used once for the combination, that was, let's see... over 700 possible combinations. That would take a while to punch in.

They couldn't expect him to figure out the code by trial and error, so there had to be some other way, or some pattern. He punched the keys in order, and nothing happened. He tried them in reverse order, with no luck, then tried odds followed by evens, and evens followed by odds.

He was starting to get frustrated. What did his dad always say? Work smarter, not harder.

Jake closed his eyes and visualized the keypad. It was laid out just like the keypad on a phone — and most numbers on a phone were also associated with letters. He knew which letters went with which numbers from years of texting, so maybe he should be trying to spell something to open the door. The pads for 1 and 0 weren't used, and they were the only numbers that didn't have letters on a phone keypad, so he thought he was on to something. But then he realized, the only letters he couldn't use were P, Q, R, S, W, X, Y, and Z — which left a whole lot of possible words. He couldn't spell "Stormglass" with no S, and "Hale" didn't have enough letters, and —

He opened his eyes. What had Jenny shouted back when he asked her what the combination was?

"Good luck!"

Jake quickly punched in the numbers 4, 6, 6, 3, 5, 8, 2, and 5 – the ones that spelled "Good luck."

The door buzzed and swung open, and Jake stepped through.

Inside was a room of doors. Literally, the inner walls were covered in doors and locks. It was like being in some weird story about portals to other universes. There was no one inside, though.

Jake *hmmed*, wondering if this was another test. Did he have to figure out the right door to open? He tried a few, but they were all locked.

Then an ordinary wooden door creaked open, and a young man stepped through. He was in his twenties, with wavy black hair pulled into a ponytail, dressed in a black turtleneck and black pants covered in zippers. He carried a dark gray toolbox.

"Agent Hale," he said, voice soft enough that Jake had to listen close to make out the words. "I am Snakesman. I have only a few hours to teach you the basics of surreptitious entry and interrogation." He shook his head, almost sadly. "It's not enough time for either, but we'll make do."

He knelt and opened his toolbox. "There are two ways to enter a place where you are not welcome. The ugly way, and the secret way." He removed a short metal crowbar from the toolbox and held it up to the light. "This is the ugly way. You jam a pry bar between a door and the frame, shove, break it open, and enter. It is very fast, but — of course — leaves a mark."

He gestured to a door that had been obviously opened with a crowbar. The lock was practically wrenched from the wood, and jagged splintered edges showed where the tool had been used.

"It is not secret. It is not surreptitious. Instead, I will teach you how to enter without a key, and without leaving a trace."

Snakesman smiled as he started to show Jake how to pick locks, using the myriad locked doors to demonstrate. He showed Jake how to use different types of picks — diamond picks, single-balls, rake picks — and demonstrated how they were used to solve different sorts of problems.

But then Snakesman brushed aside the pile of picks. "Now that you know the basics, I can tell you: you will not be using picks. Instead, you will use these." He tore open the bottom section of his toolbox to reveal drawers of paper clips, safety pins, hair clips, staples, tweezers, screwdrivers and Allen wrenches.

They sat at a table covered in locks, and Snakesman set Jake to work, using only the improvised tools at his disposal. Occasionally Snakesman made suggestions and corrected his technique, but he was clearly impressed with the speed at which Jake learned. Jake grew completely absorbed in defeating one particular lock, and was surprised when Snakesman tapped him on the shoulder and said, "Surreptitious entry's time is up, for now."

"Can I take this lock with me? So I can practice?" Jake said.

Snakesman's lips twitched into an appreciative smile. "Of course. But first, we need to discuss deception. Listen carefully. What I'm about to tell you could someday save your life. Now, I want you to picture an event, a place, a time, that's either real or imagined."

Jake frowned. "Uh, I guess it's—"

"Don't describe it, just picture it."

Shrugging, Jake started to imagine a towering blue brontosaurus — but he was barely picturing it when Snakesman whispered, "You're lying."

"But I barely started!"

Snakesman smiled and nodded.

"The power of a secret agent, Hale."

"You just guessed," Jake said, realizing Snakesman had a fifty-fifty chance of getting it right.

"Okay, Hale. Try it again."

Jake imagined something five times, and each time Snakesman called it as true or false. Each time, he was right.

"You're right handed, Jake. When right-handed people make up a place or an event, they look up and to the left — just as you did each time you imagined a lie. When you remembered something you'd seen, you looked up and to the right. Left-handed people do the opposite. Use this in interviews. If you're asking someone what they saw, are they remembering it, or inventing it? Are they telling the truth or a lie? Practice, Agent Hale. Try it with Filby and Lizzie... but be warned, they've practiced lying too."

Jake tried to keep his face blank. He wondered if he could read lies using these tricks. He wished he'd been able to use these tricks on the guy with the gun.

"The Vindiqo agent who held a gun on you," Snakesman said, and Jake gasped. *Had he been reading Jake's mind?* "He was about my age, yes?"

"I guess," Jake said, confused.

Snakesman nodded. "The scar on his face, it was like this?" Snakesman used his finger to draw a line down his own face, from his right temple down to the corner of his mouth. Jake nodded.

"His name is Mundt," Snakesman said with a growl. "I know him. I know him well. Watch out for him. He's nasty. Known for demolitions – that's how he lost his arm."

Jake gasped, then remembered. "But this man had both arms—"

"Yes. He does now. But a few years back, a sabotaged detonator tore one off in a blast. Now one is real, and one is horribly artificial. Strong enough to crush stones, I hear. Another piece of shrapnel took off half his face — the scar is where doctors sewed it back on." He looked at his hands, thinking. "But that's neither here nor there. Agent Hale, there's something important I need from you."

"What's that?"

"I need for you to meet The Colonel," Snakesman said, pushing a button under the table.

MOLE HUNT

Colonel Rex stepped into the room.

The leader of Stormglass was older than Jake's own parents, maybe even as old as his grandparents, with short gray hair and a small beard. "Welcome, Agent Hale," he said, and his voice was British, much like the Beekeeper's. He sounded like someone Jake might hear on the radio.

The Colonel stood with his hands clasped behind his back, looking at Jake sternly, then turned to Snakesman. "I'll take it from here." Snakesman nodded and left, as the Colonel sat down in his chair.

"This meeting is unusual," he said. "I don't generally meet agents in person until well after they've completed their training, but these are unfortunate times. I require your help, Agent Hale."

Jake sat up straighter.

"I have reason to believe that we have a mole in our organization."

"A mole," Jake said. The word was familiar from spy movies his dad had picked on movie nights. "You mean, like, a double agent? Someone working for the enemy, but pretending to work for Stormglass?"

The Colonel nodded. "Exactly. Ever since you joined us, Vindiqo has been one step ahead of us."

"What do you mean?"

"The twins at the park, and then again at the dead drop," the Colonel said.

"But they followed us!"

"And the man at your safe house?"

Jake scrunched up his face. "He... he must have followed us too!"

"And then the attack in England?"

Jake gulped. It did sound suspicious.

"I've suspected a leak, but my suspicions have only grown stronger."

"I swear it wasn't me, I'd never even heard of Vindiqo before a few days ago. Or Stormglass!"

"I know. But how else could Vindiqo have known," the Colonel asked sadly, studying his hands. He took a deep breath. "You see, only three other people knew about these meetings." Jake's stomach tensed, as he realized he already knew what the Colonel was going to say. "Your Echelon Leader knew, and so did Lizzie and Filby."

"But... but that's... how can that be possible? No, the twins followed us from the park, that's how they found the dead drop. It wasn't Lizzie or Filby. It couldn't have been! Maybe, maybe, what if it was Jenny?"

"It's possible," Colonel Rex admitted, "and we're watching her, but I want you to help us by watching Lizzie and Filby."

"I don't believe it!" Jake pushed himself back from the table, on the verge of anger. "They're both my friends, and I've seen them in the field, and they're — they love Stormglass!"

"I understand." Rex bowed his head and used a finger to trace along the tabletop. "And I agree with you. I do hope that I'm wrong. But if there is a spy in our midst, I need to know before any of our agents get killed. Before you get killed."

The Colonel rose, started toward the door, then paused. "This is a lot to ask of any young agent, but I do need your help. Can you offer me that?"

"I guess I have to," Jake said sullenly. *It's got to be Jenny*, he thought to himself, *if it's anybody at all.*

Jake watched as the Colonel left, closing the door behind him. He sat for a while, thinking hard, then bit his lip and realized he really had no choice.

MISSION OF DESTRUCTION

"That's it!" Jenny cried, stretching out her arms and smiling widely. "You've completed the fastest crash-course in spycraft ever."

"I feel ready," Jake said.

Jenny cocked her head. "You seem upset. Is there something you're not telling me?"

Jake remained stone-faced, but felt his heart beating louder. "No."

Jenny leaned in, and spoke slowly. "Are you sure?"

Jake shook his head, unwilling to even breathe. *Was she going to try to recruit him to spy for Vindiqo?* He tried to read her body language, to look at where she was looking, and all the other stuff Snakesman had taught him. Could she really be a double agent?

"Well, it's dinner time! So let's get moving!"

Jake exhaled.

After filling their trays with spaghetti and meat balls and garlic bread, Jenny led Jake toward the back of the dining hall, which was full of the buzz and hum of conversation of young agents.

Jake brightened when he saw Lizzie and Filby sitting at a small table in the corner, and they waved at him, Lizzie grinning. There was no way they could be working for Vindiqo! Maybe there was no leak at all, or Vindiqo had some kind of secret surveillance program the Colonel didn't know about...

Jenny and Jake sat down with the others. "How's it going, new kid?" Lizzie said. "Are you a fully-fledged superspy yet?"

"I'm getting there," Jake said with a grin. "What have you guys been up to?"

"Oh, just brushing up on some skills," Lizzie said. "I'm this close to my scuba certification. I'll be swimming around underwater with bomb-sniffing dolphins within a couple of months, you just wait and see."

Filby shook his head. "Sounds cold. I like my swimming pools heated."

"Since when do you like any kind of swimming pool?" said Lizzie, looking pointedly at the two desserts Filby had helped himself to.

"Very funny, Lizzie," said Filby sarcastically. "Anyway, more importantly, I've been down in the labs, helping the researchers develop weapons to use against the bees."

"Weapons," Lizzie said. "Awesome!"

"And I got to see the Colonel," Filby said. "He wanted to meet you, Hale, but he said your training was too important."

Jake ate a meatball to keep himself from saying anything he shouldn't — *the Colonel gave me a special mission* — and just tried to look disappointed instead. Although every time he thought about the special

135

mission, he did feel disappointed. "What did the Colonel talk to you about?"

"Oh, just how the fate of the world hangs in the balance," Filby said. "How this is the most important mission we've ever been assigned. Things like that."

Lizzie glanced at Jenny. "Of course, if someone would tell us what the mission actually is..."

"Once you're all done eating, we'll go to the briefing room and talk about it," Jenny said.

Filby, Lizzie, and Jake all dropped their forks at the same time, and chorused, "Done," more or less in one voice.

Jenny giggled. "That's the kind of eagerness we like to see. Come on, then."

They sat in a dim room like a movie theater, with a screen at the front, but with only about eight seats. Jenny fiddled with her Stormpad and a map appeared onscreen, displaying North and South America, then zoomed in on a red-highlighted portion of South America that covered almost the whole bottom half of the continent.

"Argentina," Jenny said. "The second-largest country in South America. A million square miles, ranging from rough mountain terrain to fertile valleys. It's also one of the world's biggest honey exporters. Our intelligence indicates that Vindiqo has a secret outpost in the southern Andes Mountains, and while we can't be sure, we suspect they've got a lab there, developing bees."

The image on the screen changed again, showing a satellite picture of rectangular buildings nestled in mountains. "This is a Vindiqo factory," she said. "It's supposed to be a soybean processing plant, but intel suggests it's actually something else."

"We want to know what they're up to. Are they creating more bees? If so, what are the bees going to be used for? We'll be dropping you three in a position to the north, hopefully beyond their area of surveillance. Your cover, in case you're spotted, is you're high school kids on a camping expedition. You've lost the rest of your troop. Details and your cover names are in the mission briefing." She passed out three folders. "Memorize them and destroy the documents. And whatever you do, do not enter the base. If there's something illegal going on, contact me and we'll discuss possible options."

She handed them each a small case, about a hand's-width wide. "To help with surveillance, we'll provide each of you with one of these. These are the latest version of our flying bugs. They're small, quiet, and fast, and they can transmit video and audio back to your Stormpads. Get close to the facility and send these gadgets flying in to get a better look — especially inside the buildings, if possible. Once we know what we're dealing with, we'll send in reinforcements. And Filby, you've got the bombs, right?"

"Bombs?" Lizzie gasped with excitement.

"Pheromone bombs," Filby said.

"Brutal," Lizzie said, as Filby handed them out.

"What's a pheromone?" asked Jake.

"It's the way bees communicate," said Jenny. "Different pheromones have different smells, and one might mean, *hello chaps, there's nectar over here*." All three agents stifled laughs at her terrible English accent. She sounded like she was impersonating the Beekeeper. "Sorry, aren't bees British? Anyhow, there are other pheromones that say 'send doctors,' or 'follow me.' The pheromones in these bombs are called the Attack Pheromone — they'll make Vindiqo bees attack other Vindiqo bees. There's also a poison mixed in, which won't hurt humans but will slowly kill off any remaining bees."

"Sweet," Lizzie said, handling one of the small bombs.

"They're just for self-defense," Jenny warned. "And only if you absolutely need to use them."

"Are you sure we can't just blow the whole place up?" Lizzie shouted gleefully.

"Remember Lizzie, this trip is only about gathering intelligence," Jenny said, glaring. "We'll fly you out tonight, and you'll parachute in after dark—"

"Parachute?" Jake blurted. "You want me to jump out of a plane?" He couldn't decide if the idea was terrifying or awesome. "I... they didn't teach me how to do that."

"Don't worry about it, Hale, I've got you," Lizzie said. "No way I'll let you crash into the side of a mountain. Filby got stuck in a tree last time, but was high enough that the wolves couldn't reach him, no matter how high they jumped."

"Wolves?" Jake echoed.

"Don't worry, Hale," Jenny said. "There are no wolves in the Andes."

"Just giant condors," Filby added nervously. "Ten-foot wingspans. Try not to hit any of those on your way down."

"Any more questions before we wrap this up?" asked Jenny.

The room was brimming with excitement, but Jake had one nagging concern.

"What about the beekeeper," he asked. "Is he okay?"

"He lost all his bees," said Jenny. "Even without the fire and the poison, he would have. The invaders took over his hives and killed the queens. It seems like the first thing they did."

"The bees invaded his hives," said Jake. "Were they meant to do that?"

"It's a good question, and we're still trying to work that one out," said Jenny. "Now, I think it's time all three of you go get some sleep. I know it's not bedtime yet, but—"

"Sleep when you can," they chorused.

Jenny nodded. "We'll wake you in a few hours for the trip. You hang back for a minute, Hale."

Lizzie and Filby looked at Jake curiously before saying good night and leaving the room. Jenny waited until the others were out of range, and then turned to Jake with her usual big smile. Jake started to feel like

TIM PRATT AND ANDY DEEMER

Jenny's smile was hiding something, but he wasn't sure if this was his imagination. Clearly, spying on his fellow agents was going to be exhausting.

"Now I know you're a fan of coin tricks," Jenny said, as she scooped a handful of coins from her pocket. "So I picked up some change for you — *for a change.*" She smirked at her own bad joke as she handed them over, one by one. "These are from the tech lab. The half-dollars, these, are bugs. Slip one in someone's pocket and tune in with your Stormpad! You'll hear whatever they say."

Jake gasped, as she dropped several more into his palm.

"And these are flash-bang grenades," she said.

Jake jumped back. "These are grenades?!"

"No, no, no," laughed Jenny. "Flash-bang grenades. They're like stun grenades, they'll flash light and make a wild noise, and disorient everyone else around. Just give one a twist clockwise, a timer will start, and you've got thirty seconds before it goes off. Or give it a twist counter-clockwise and it'll go off immediately. BOOM!"

She dropped two more coins into his hand. "These will create distractions. I don't remember which is which — sorry! — but one will play incredible battle noises like gunfire and shouting, and the other will play the sound of a man screaming and crying for help. And they're really loud."

Jake looked down at his handful of fake coins, and smiled. *Spy gadgets, for him!* "These are awesome," he cried.

Okay, so maybe one of his fellow agents was a traitor, and maybe he was going to have to jump out of a plane soon, and maybe there were murderous bees and deadly criminals arrayed against him — but he was having fun.

STARBUSTER

"This is Hangar X," Lizzie said, spinning around in the vast space, arms outstretched. Jake realized he was staring open-mouthed. He'd been to airports before, and seen lots of planes, even fighter jets at an air show, but he'd never seen planes like these. No two were alike — some had four wings, and some looked like nothing more than a wing. There were huge, needle-nosed black jets and tiny one-man ultralights. One fighter jet had giant fans in the middle of its wings, and another had wings that seemed to be put on backwards. Lizzie led them to a plane at one end of the hangar.

"When you've got a need for speed," she said, patting the side, "you can't do better than the Starbuster." The plane was about 40 feet long, and looked like a fighter jet with a needlepointed nose. "It'll hit Mach 2, and get us to Argentina in four or five hours."

"Are you going to fly this?" Jake said, amazed.

"I wish. I'm not even certified yet. It's going to be autonomous."

"Like Hermes? You mean the plane won't have a pilot?"

"Yeah, isn't that cool!"

Lizzie mounted a metal set of stairs to the open cockpit, where there were three seats in a row. Jake nervously took the back seat, with Filby in the middle, and Lizzie up front. She made sure they were all strapped in before she turned on the plane's communications system. "We're all set. Let her rip."

Lizzie whooped as the cockpit bubble closed over them. The plane rumbled forward, up a steep incline, and then suddenly shot out into the desert, emerging from a bay door concealed in a pile of boulders. Jake tilted his head back and looked at the clear, bright stars overhead. "Prepare for takeoff," Lizzie said.

The jet engines kicked in with a deafening roar, and Jake felt as if a giant hand was pressing against his chest, trying to shove him through the back of the plane. He gasped as they hurtled forward, and his stomach dropped when they went airborne. Tears streamed from his eyes, and he clutched the arms of his seat, irrationally afraid of falling. He looked up again, expecting the stars to be streaking past the way they did on TV when spaceships went to warp speed, but they just continued shining down as the trio shot through the night.

"WHOOOOOO!" Lizzie shouted, as they, impossibly, went even faster.

"Can you not scream into my ear like that?" Filby said.

"Hold on tight, boys," Lizzie said. "It's going to be quite a ride."

Even the novelty of hurtling along at insane speeds through the darkness faded after an hour or so, and Jake took out his Stormpad and listened to Storm tell him everything the computer could about Vindiqo and his instructors — Jake's level three security clearance opened up a whole new shelf of information, and he did his best to absorb it all.

Eventually the hours passed and the plane descended, fast, and landed at an airfield in the dark. The landing was as bumpy as riding a bicycle down a potholed road, but at least it was over quickly. Once the Starbuster slowed to a stop, the cockpit cracked open, and Jake sucked in great gasping lungfuls of cold, fresh air. He hadn't realized how stale the pressurized air in the Starbuster had become.

They climbed out of the aircraft — Lizzie sliding down the banister of the portable stairs, Filby and Jake both wobbling their way down — dragging their backpacks after them. The ground crew didn't speak to them, but handed over bottles of water, which the young agents gratefully chugged. Jake looked around, but in the dark, there wasn't much to see: just rugged mountains, metal sheds, and men and women moving around the airfield purposefully.

The agents took a few minutes to use the bathroom in the small office — one of the most disgusting toilets Jake had ever seen, and he didn't dare to wash his hands, afraid just touching the sink would make him even filthier. Filby passed him a small bottle of hand sanitizer wordlessly. Once they were done, the ground crew hustled them back outside, past the Starbuster, and over to a second small runway. The plane waiting for them there was bigger, older, and painted dark green, with propellers instead of jet engines.

"That's the one we jump out of," Filby said, nervously.

"I love these ugly old planes," Lizzie said, shouting a little — their ears were still pretty beat up from hours in a roaring jet. "You can fix them with wrenches, and oilcans, and rubber bands and wire. New planes are all computers, and you can't make a computer work by hitting it with a hammer."

"Give me computers anytime," Filby said.

The back of the plane was open, with a ramp leading up from the ground, and they all walked inside. The interior was pretty much just plain metal, with long benches running along the walls. The pilot greeted them in Spanish — which both Filby and Lizzie seemed to speak — and showed Lizzie where the parachutes were. She helped Filby into his gear, and then helped Jake. The parachute pack — surprisingly heavy — went onto his back, and Lizzie showed him how to wear the backpack with his gear backwards on his chest. "Don't worry," she said. "I'll walk you through the whole process, and I'll be right there with you for the jump."

The pilot said something, and Lizzie brightened. "Oh, sweet! Filby, we're getting welbikes."

"Beats walking through the Andes, I guess," he said. "Though I could use a little break from all this speed."

Lizzie stood with her arms crossed, glaring at him.

"If you're tired of moving fast, Filby, you're tired of life."

THE JUMP

The plane was so much slower than the Starbuster that Jake half expected it to fall out of the sky. After what seemed like a very short time, though, the pilot shouted to Lizzie. She stood up. "All right, boys, we're almost over the jump site. Hale, do exactly what I tell you, when I tell you, and maybe you won't get mushed against the side of a mountain. Filby, you're on your own. Go ahead and take care of the Welbikes!"

"Yes, boss," he cried over the noise. He detached himself from the wall and pushed a refrigerator-sized crate on wheels toward the back of the plane. The cargo door swung open, letting in the roar of a vast wind, and Filby shoved the crate out of the plane. Then he pulled his goggles down over his eyes, turned around, gave a little wave, and jumped out of the plane himself. No hesitation at all. Maybe it was like jumping into a cold pool, Jake thought, with a tense and nervous knot in his stomach. If you tried to go in slowly, you'd never go at all. Better to just take the plunge.

Lizzie had explained the idea behind tandem jumping on their walk to Hangar X. She would wear a special harness, with attachments on the front that would attach his back to her chest. They'd jump out of the plane together, with Lizzie controlling everything, while Jake dangled off her front.

"Like a baby in a sling?" he'd asked, embarrassed.

"Not even remotely," she said. "Almost everyone does their first skydive this way." Now Lizzie attached her harness to Jake's, maneuvered them toward the open ramp — he was too nervous to move himself — and she shouted in his ear. "Ready? Set? JUMP!"

They leapt out together, and began falling. The sensation was incredible, the wind rushing past his ears in a roar. There was no weight of Lizzie on his back, no real pull from the straps, and Lizzie whooped with delight behind him.

"Amazing, isn't it?" Lizzie shouted into Jake's ears. His face was too stretched and contorted by the wind to talk, but he was laughing deliriously inside. It felt like he'd leaned his head out of a speeding car, with the wind whipping away at him — but seeing the ground so far away was simply unreal. Jake spread his arms out and imagined he was flying as clouds whipped by. The ground below was just a shadowland of greater and lesser darkness, every mountain peak so small it looked fake.

After a few moments of delirious, delicious free fall, Lizzie triggered the chute, and Jake felt a hard jerk against his shoulders and across his chest, everywhere the harness was secured. He whipped from facedown to upright, and the two of them floated down together calmly towards the earth. Lizzie steered, shifting their black parachute this way and that by tugging on wires, and aiming them for the landing zone they'd prepared for. The ground now resolved itself into mountains, hills, and trees, and suddenly everything seemed a lot bigger and rougher and harder than it had before.

"Legs up!" Lizzie shouted as the ground approached, and they slammed down and slid a few feet before Lizzie cut the parachute loose. She disconnected their harnesses from one another and shrugged out of hers. "You did good, new kid," she said quietly. "I tandem jumped with one new agent who freaked out so hard he wet himself."

"Ew," Jake said. He looked around in the darkness. "Where's Filby?"

"How'd you know that story was about Filby," she said with a snigger, then turned on a pen flashlight, rifled through her backpack and pulled out two pairs of night-vision goggles. "I hope he's not stuck in a tree again."

As he slipped on the goggles, the world became visible again, but in a strange greenish version of itself. It was disorienting, but Jake adapted quickly, racing after Lizzie across the stony, uneven ground.

"He's over there," Lizzie whispered, and pointed toward a heap of tumbled boulders some twenty feet high. Filby stood at the bottom, arms crossed over his chest, gazing upward.

"What's up?" Lizzie said.

Filby laughed, but not like he thought anything was funny. "*Up.* Yeah, that's the problem. The crate with our bikes landed up there." He pointed to the pile of rocks. "And judging from the map, it'd be a long walk without them."

"Huh," Lizzie said. "Give me a minute." Without another word, she started scrambling up the rocks. There were plenty of handholds, but the whole heap looked pretty unstable to Jake, and he and Filby both backed up, afraid of getting squashed if the rubble collapsed.

"She's going to get herself killed one day," Filby said, watching her. "But every day she doesn't get killed, she just gets that much crazier."

A few minutes later, there was a huge crash, and Filby winced. "We're supposed to be secret agents."

The crate was on the ground now, partly broken open. Lizzie came clambering down the rock heap, dropping lightly to her feet at the bottom. "See?" she said. "Perfect."

"Assuming nothing got smashed," Filby said with a growl. He started to pry open the crate's lid.

"So, welbikes," Jake said. "Are they, like, mountain bikes?"

"Not at all," Lizzie said, excited. "They're more like small folding motorbikes!"

"They were invented for paratroopers in World War Two," said Filby. "They were made so that you could be moving about ten seconds after the parachute lands. That doesn't account for when the crates land on boulders, of course."

Lizzie coughed as she rolled one of the welbikes out of the crate. "Hey — this isn't a bike at all!" It looked more like a go-kart, with four big tires and a low-slung seat. "Cool! It's a welquad!"

Filby took out his Stormpad and connected to headquarters. "We're on the ground, about to head for the lab." He listened to his earpiece for a moment, then powered down the tablet. "No changes on their end," he said. "Let's get going."

Jake and Lizzie pushed their welquads out of the crate. The controls were incredibly simple — one lever for going forward and reverse, another for the brakes. Most of the video games Jake had played were harder to operate. Finally, Jake felt in control — unlike when he was hurtling through the sky in the Starbuster, or strapped to Lizzie's chest jumping from a plane.

Lizzie and Filby raced ahead, and Jake took up rear, their little quads zipping almost silently through the mountains. Clearly Lizzie had memorized the path. The green tint of the mountains in night vision made Jake feel like he was moving through an alien landscape. His sense of direction was pretty good, but it was nothing compared to Lizzie's, and he was glad she was the one leading the way. They rolled through the silent night, swerving left and right to avoid rocks, when Jake hit a snag.

His welquad caught an outcropping of rock that Lizzie and Filby had both avoided, and he slammed to a stop as the two of them disappeared over a ridge. His quad wouldn't move, just buzzed and rocked when he tried to push the lever forward, so Jake climbed out, squatted by the back wheel, and saw the rock jammed against the rear axle. Maybe if he backed up, he could swing around the obstruction —

All of a sudden, light glared over the ridge. It was blinding, and Jake whipped the night vision goggles from his eyes. In a gut reaction, he started forward toward the light, and then immediately realized how stupid that was. He ducked off the path instead, darting to the left behind the rocks. He crawled down to his belly, heart pounding, and peered over the ridgeline.

Lizzie and Filby stood in a circle of light, surrounded by three trucks with glaring floodlights mounted on their roofs. A man's voice shouted out, "Why, it's children! How nice of you to visit."

"Thank goodness," Filby shouted excitedly. "You've found us!"

He's excited, thought Jake, a sick stone in his stomach, *is he the traitor?*

"I told you they'd find us," shouted Lizzie. "We thought we were completely lost!"

That's right, Jake thought, embarrassed. *They're sticking to the cover story.*

"You were lost," said the man in the truck. "And now you've been found. And I'm sure Stormglass will pay handsomely for your safe return."

"Storm—who? What are you talking about?" said Lizzie, less convincingly.

"Shut up, little girl. Friedman! Walker! Shove them in the trucks!"

Soldiers held guns at Lizzie and Filby while others tied them up. They'd rolled right into an ambush, and been captured. It was only dumb luck that Jake hadn't been caught, too.

"Wait! There were supposed to be three! Where's the other boy?" One of the men grabbed Lizzie, and reached back to slap her.

"No, don't harm her yet! The Doctor wants to see them first. Don't look so frightened little ones, you'll be fine. And your missing friend, well, he'll either die of starvation, or he'll die of thirst, or perhaps he'll just die from bullet wounds."

The man shouted into the night.

"If you're out there, little boy, we'll find you!"

Jake heard the tramp of at least a dozen boots moving up the ridge, and scrambled. He needed a better place to hide.

HALE TO THE RESCUE

Jake peered out from under the rock where he was hidden, watching the soldier's feet. He was so close he could have reached out and grabbed the man's ankle. But that probably wouldn't be a very good idea. This was the perfect hiding place, underneath a shelf of stone, just big enough for Jake to squeeze beneath and disappear completely. The man dropped a cigarette butt and squashed it under his boot heel, kicking up a flurry of dirt. Jake fought the urge to sneeze until the soldier moved on. They'd found his welquad and taken it away, so they knew he was around here somewhere, but he didn't think they'd expect to find him so close by.

The hardest part was waiting. He didn't dare try to contact Stormglass, not when the soldiers might hear him. After nearly an hour of lying on his belly on the stony ground, the truck engines started up and rumbled away. He wriggled out of the crack, just poking his head out of the hole. From his position on the ridgeline, he could watch the trucks departing. It was nearly dawn, the sky growing lighter, when the three vehicles disappeared in a cloud of dust. And he was entirely alone.

Either Vindiqo was very lucky, or someone had tipped them off about the mission. Jake thought about calling Jenny, but if she was the traitor, he'd be putting himself in danger. He was scared and tired and hungry, too.

So when he was sure all the soldiers were gone, he took out his Stormpad and slipped in the earpiece. He powered up the tablet, waited for it to establish a connection with the satellite, then tapped the icon that would put him through directly to Colonel Rex.

The screen shimmered, and Rex's face appeared. "Hale? Do you have news to report already?"

"Not exactly," Jake said. "I mean, I don't know who the traitor is. But Filby and Lizzie have been caught. I'm hiding in the desert, but I don't know what to do!"

"Hale?"

"Wait, can't you hear me?"

"Hale, I can't hear you. You're breaking up. There seems to be interf-"

The connection went dark. Jake tried again, but it wouldn't connect, and he tried again, and it wouldn't connect — so he placed his hands over his face, and silently yelled into the dawn. How had he gotten into this mess? Days ago he was bored, wishing something — anything! — would happen. Now he was lost and abandoned in the desert, hunted by the armed guards of some insane evil corporation. He fought back tears, and anger, and frustration, and then he remembered his dad. He wiped a dirty tear away. Work smarter, he thought. He looked in his satchel. He had food and water, but he was still thousands of miles from home.

The sun was starting to come up, and Jake knew he would be easily visible from the air. He thought back to his two days of training, and rolled around in the dirt, making himself gray and dusty all over. He would blend in better with the landscape this way. Then he scurried from one piece of cover to the next, moving slowly over the broken ground, following the track but staying well away from it. He knew that would lead him to the base; and the base was his greatest fear, and his only chance of survival.

After an hour of walking, he saw a group of long, low buildings in the distance, the same gray as the mountains, surrounded by a tall fence. A couple of armed men guarded the front gate, and another walked the perimeter. This must be the base.

Jake found a good observation position, on top of a rock outcropping, and went down flat on his belly. A giant condor flew in long, lazy circles high above him, its vast wings casting long, slanted shadows on Jake's back. He plugged in his earpiece, and tried his Stormpad again. It worked, but there was still no connection to headquarters. Clearly something was jamming that signal.

He took off his backpack and removed the box that contained the flying bug. It was a delicate, spindly thing with paddle-shaped wings, vaguely resembling a dragonfly. The drones weren't modeled on bees, he thought gratefully. He didn't know if he could face another bee right now.

After activating his Stormpad and opening up the control software, he pushed the flying bug off the rock. Its wings buzzed, and it took to the air, hovering. Jake looked at the screen of his Stormpad, which displayed the drone's wide-angle camera view. At least this connection still worked. Using the touchscreen controls, he guided the flying bug forward, sending it down into the valley, buzzing up to pass over the fence and around the facility.

He flew the drone over the flat metal roofs of the buildings, tanks that probably held fuel or water, and pickup trucks parked on concrete. *Where are Lizzie and Filby*, Jake wondered. He steered the drone lower and went buzzing around in search of an open window, without much luck, and then saw a door open up in the side of the largest building. A soldier dressed in a gray jumpsuit was coming outside.

With deft videogame-honed hand movements, Jake steered the bug over and through the door just before it swung shut. The drone wouldn't pass for an insect up close, but he was lucky so far — the first room was empty, nothing but a battered metal desk and a couple of chairs and filing cabinets. The table was covered in papers, but he couldn't focus close enough to read them. Jake flew the dragonfly down a hallway, which was lined with rows of large metal canisters or drums of some kind, and ended in a closed door. The door had a square glass window in the middle, so he hovered the bug in front of it, and worked the camera zoom and focus to see the space beyond.

The room held rows upon rows of white towers, like the wooden beehives Jake had seen in England.

Half a dozen people moved around in full beekeeper outfits, complete with bulky gloves and boots. Some of them draped the hives in heavy netting, and others moved the boxes on hand trucks toward the back of the building...

"Watch it," screamed a voice into Jake's earpiece. He jerked the drone down, saving it from being crushed behind an opening door. "Drop one hive and it's over for all of us! Please, be more careful! Remember these are killers!"

Jake was confused: "over for all of us"? These men were already dressed in bee suits — wouldn't that protect them? But perhaps these bees were even more poisonous than the ones from England. He set the drone on auto-hover, and took out his binoculars. He focused them until he had a clear, close-up view of the pickup trucks parked at the back of the large building.

"Oh crud," Jake said under his breath. Men were out there now, dressed in beekeeper uniforms, loading the netted hives onto the trucks. Where were they taking the bees?

Jake thought back to what the Beekeeper had said, and the mission briefing, and what little he knew. These bees may have been trained to kill, and may be filled with poison. These beekeepers were definitely prepping the hives for transport. Were they going to unleash the bees on Argentina, or were they just moving them to a new location because they'd been discovered? It looked like everything was being cleared out, which would include Lizzie and Filby.

Jake knew there wasn't time to wait for reinforcements. He had to rescue his friends.

There were only two other buildings, and they must be trapped in one of them. If he could get the drone back outside, perhaps he could find them. Jake picked up the Stormpad again. But the screen didn't show the room anymore. Instead, it featured a man's face — middle-aged, clean-shaven, with steel-blue eyes peering out from round-rimmed glasses. "Hello, little bug," the man said into Jake's earpiece. His eyebrows were immense, shaggy white things, like some bizarre form of arctic caterpillar adapted to hide in the snow. "And hello, little detective. We thought you ran away. You really should have, you know."

Before Jake could take control of the drone, the man had grabbed it. "I'm busy now, but there's no rush. You're such a long way from anyone who can help you." He looked to his right and screamed, "He's out there! Get him!" Voices replied in unison, several calling him Doctor. He slowly turned back to the camera. "I so look forward to meeting you," he said, "So I can teach you a lesson you'll never forget." The screen suddenly buzzed and went black. The drone was gone.

Jake thought fast. He'd only have a few minutes before they started looking for him. He thought about how killer bees invaded hives — the toughest defenders were always right at the entrance, but once the invaders got inside, there were nothing but harmless drones who couldn't put up a fight. Just like a hive, there were armed guards at the gate, but the beekeepers loading the trucks weren't carrying guns. Jake might actually be safer if he could get inside the fence... But how?

Then he remembered his trick coins.

He took the golden coin from his pocket, twisted it, and threw it as hard and far as he could. The coin arced high, flashing in the sun, and landed beyond a heap of rocks. A few moments later, he heard a man begin to scream and cry, begging for help. The gate guards looked at each other, then bolted toward the sound. The perimeter guard started for it as well.

Jake put his head down and ran. He skimmed down to the fence, grabbed a pair of wire cutters from his pocket, and cut a gap just small enough to wriggle through. Then he rushed to the nearest building and huddled against the side. The coin was still screaming, but then trailed off — before the guards found it, Jake hoped. Better if they didn't realize they'd fallen for a distraction.

Keeping his back to the wall, he edged along quickly. Unzipping one of his pockets, he removed a small mirror on a long handle, and used it to peek around the corner. Nobody in sight. He scurried around, and discovered the door was chained shut and fastened with a padlock.

Jake rattled the chain, and a voice shouted out, "Stay away — we're dangerous!" It was Filby!

ACCIDENTAL INTEL

"It's me," Jake whispered through the crack at the door.

"Hale?" Lizzie said. "Amazing! We need to move fast. Can you get the lock open?"

"Working on it." He hunched his shoulders, hoping no one would come around the side of the building before he finished. He bent a paperclip into shape, slipped it into the lock, then slid in a hair clip, trying to feel the tiny changes in pressure as he pushed up the pins in the lock. If only he could have practiced more... Then again, this was practice, wasn't it? And he definitely had motivation. *One down.* A bead of sweat ran down his forehead. *Two down.* He thought he heard footsteps, but ignored them as they moved away. *Three down.*

Done. Once he felt the last pin shift, he removed the hair clip and twisted the paper clip. The padlock clicked open, and Jake eased the chain from between the door handles. He ducked inside the shed, where Lizzie and Filby were tied up, lying on a pile of sacks. Lizzie bent around to show Jake her wrists, bound behind her with plastic zip ties.

This obviously wasn't a place Vindiqo had planned to use as a holding cell — it was more of a storage shed. Tools hung on the walls, and shelves were covered in bottles of chemicals and assorted beekeeping supplies, including a pair of beekeeper suits, complete with hoods and veils.

Jake ran over to Lizzie, drew a pocketknife, and sawed through the ties around her ankles and wrists, then moved on to Filby.

"What's happening out there?" she asked. "We didn't see anything at all."

Jake gave them a quick rundown on what he'd seen, and they were clearly alarmed when he mentioned the trucks being loaded. "Do you have the smoke bombs?" Lizzie asked.

Jake nodded, and with some effort pulled the cluster of smoke bombs from his bag. The bombs were cylindrical, and each one had a digital timer. Lizzie took them all, then reconsidered and gave a few back to Jake.

"If they've blocked communications and they're loading the trucks," Lizzie said, "we can't wait for backup. We have to act now."

Filby nodded.

"But," Jake said, feeling like it was too late to be stating the obvious, "What can three kids do against an army?"

Lizzie and Filby glared at him.

"Three kids couldn't do much," she said, "but we're not just kids. We're agents. We're Stormglass agents. This is what we were trained to do." She grabbed one of the beekeeper suits down from the shelf. "Do you think we could pass for beekeepers?"

"Uh, I guess. There are a lot of guys dressed in those right now," Jake said. "But there are only two suits."

"Leave me here," Filby said. "Just give me your Stormpad, Hale." Jake hesitated — was it a good idea to give Filby his Stormpad, when Filby might be the traitor? "Look, the security system here is definitely computerized. Let me try to hack in while you guys are out there. I can download blueprints and maps, and find the best way out."

"Hale, log in and give it to him," urged Lizzie.

Jake couldn't refuse without a good reason, so he nodded, activated the pad with his palm print, and then passed it over. "Don't do anything bad," he murmured. Filby gave him an odd look, then focused on the pad.

Lizzie was already dressed in a beekeeper suit, looking like something out of a science fiction movie. "Hurry up, Hale." She thrust the other suit toward him.

Jake slipped into the baggy outfit, pulled on the boots and gloves, and then lowered the screened hood onto his shoulders. "I hope I don't have to do any backflips while wearing this," he said with a nervous laugh.

"You think this is bad, you should try wearing a spacesuit sometime."

"When did you ever have to wear a spacesuit?"

"Lizzie, tell him about your adventures another time." Filby was sitting on the sacks again, tapping away at Jake's Stormpad urgently. "You need to disrupt their operations. I'll meet you at the extraction point."

Lizzie peeked out the door — at least, she tried to peek, but it was hard to be subtle in a giant white suit. She pushed open the door and beckoned Jake to follow her. Once they were outside, she closed the doors and looped the chains loosely around the handle, then snapped the lock closed around a single link. At a glance, the shed still appeared secure, but the chain would slip free if Filby gave the door a good shove.

"I'll take care of the bees on the truck," she said. "You try to get into the lab, and make sure any bees they left behind get smoked out. And look for any intel. Papers, flash drives, anything. Maybe this isn't the only bee base."

"Okay. Where should I meet you?"

"At the extraction site," she said. "To the north, remember? We'll all meet there. Assuming we can make it out." She gave him a fist-pump with her oversized gloves. "Good job breaking us out, new kid." Then she turned and was gone.

Jake tried to walk purposefully, looking like he belonged, as he approached the laboratory building. Beekeepers rushed past him in a hurry. They knew Stormglass was on to them.

Jake tugged open the door and stepped into the front office, then froze. It wasn't empty anymore. A woman with long hair and a short skirt stood by one of the filing cabinets, taking out folders and papers and running them all through a shredder. She glanced at him, then looked back at her work without a word, so Jake exhaled and walked on down the hallway.

He peered through the square window in the door, and saw things had changed since his drone had been here — the hives and the beekeepers were all gone, as if they'd never been here in the first place. Jake stepped through and scanned for hidden guards or stray murder-bees, but there was nothing.

The next room was just a small office with a beat-up metal desk and equally battered filing cabinets. The desk was covered with a sprawl of messy papers, as if someone had been interrupted suddenly and left.

Jake glanced through the papers, and while he didn't have time to carefully read them, certain phrases jumped out: "eyes only," "destroy after reading," "Trans-Siberian railroad," and a date — the day after tomorrow. Other sheets were covered in groups of random numbers. Coordinates, maybe? He wasn't sure, but it looked important. Jake ripped off his gloves, unzipped his suit and fumbled around until he found his HyperOpticon, then carefully photographed each page. Once they were all captured, he meticulously put the pages back just as he'd found them and stowed the device away.

Jake looked around, but there was nothing else here. He rushed from the office, and was almost through the entrance when a scowling man appeared — the Doctor! His eyebrows were massive, and he carried a black bag slung over his shoulder. He saw Jake, and glared. "What are you doing in here?" he demanded.

Pitching his voice as low as he could, Jake said, "Making sure nothing was left behind, sir."

"I wouldn't trust any of you to secure the scene," Doctor Eyebrows roared. "You damned contractors! Soldiers who can't find one stupid child, movers who almost drop hives of killer bees! The Chairman will hear about this. Get out of here, and finish loading the trucks. We have to get out."

Jake turned away, hoping he wasn't expected to salute or something, and headed toward the stairs leading down to the loading dock.

"Wait!" Doctor Eyebrows shouted, and Jake's heart almost stopped. Had the doctor realized he was just a kid? Jake slowly turned.

Doctor Eyebrows whipped the bag off his own shoulder, and shoved it into Jake's chest. "Put this in the front seat of the first truck. It's the single most important thing you'll ever touch, so don't lose it."

"Of course," Jake said in his low voice, and exhaled as he raced toward the back doors.

The loading dock was still a hive of activity, the buzzing coming from the backs of the trucks, secured under tarps. Men and women ran to and fro, carrying equipment, coiling lengths of wire... and, in one case, splashing gasoline all around the little shed where Filby was still held captive. They were planning to burn the facility, and their hostages too! *These people were deranged!*

Someone grabbed his arm, and Jake nearly jumped. He swerved, and then recognized Lizzie inside the mesh-covered hood. She led the way around the building, away from Filby's shed, and Jake followed, hoping she knew what she was doing.

Once they were away from all the others, she whispered, "What's in the bag?"

"I don't know. Doctor Eyebrows — uh, the scientist guy in charge — he gave it to me and told me to put it in a truck. He said it's important."

"Score," Lizzie cheered quietly. "Accidental intel! Okay, let's get out of here." She started toward the fence.

"Uh, Lizzie?"

"What?"

"They're about to burn down the shed. And Filby's still in it!"

CODE BOOK

"Nah," Lizzie laughed. "Don't worry about Filby."

"Why? Is he fireproof?"

"He wishes. No, he's already out of the shed. He locked up the chain on the door so it looks like we're still inside. As long as they don't open the door to check on us before burning us alive, we should be fine."

"So where is he?"

As if on cue, a metal grate rose up at their feet, and Filby's head popped out. "Hurry up," he urged. "Assuming the other end of this tunnel isn't buried in rubble, we should be able to reach the extraction point this way!"

Descending the ladder in the beekeeper outfit was awkward for Jake, but it didn't seem to slow Lizzie down at all. He was glad to get out of the clumsy costume when he reached the bottom.

"I found our gear," Filby said to Lizzie as he hefted a pair of backpacks from the floor of the dank, low-ceilinged tunnel. "I didn't find any intel though. I couldn't risk going into the buildings."

"It's okay — Hale got some goodies. The head guy's duffel bag!"

Jake remembered his HyperOpticon. "I also found—"

"Let's just get out of this hot zone," Filby said. "Remember, this is hostile territory!" He bustled deep into the tunnel.

"Did you manage to plant the bombs?" Jake asked Lizzie as they followed behind.

"Oh, yeah," she said. "I just climbed up on the trucks, and nobody even looked at me. I set each bomb on a thirty-minute timer, right next to the hives. Any minute, those bees are gonna go crazy. I just hope this was the only laboratory they had. Wouldn't it be nice to knock out their whole supply of death bees in one morning?"

Jake wondered if she was telling the truth. And if she was telling the truth, was Filby leading them into a trap?

The tunnel soon enveloped them in total darkness — if there'd ever been lights down here, they didn't work anymore. They found their night vision goggles again, and could see in the pressing blackness, but something about the cold metal tunnels rendered in green made it even scarier. Jake splashed through damp puddles, and his feet kicked mysterious bits of trash with every step. He saw rats scuttling around too, but at least they darted away from the footsteps.

Finally a dim shaft of light appeared ahead. Another rusty metal ladder was attached to the wall, leading up to a metal grate on the surface, half-covered in rocks. Jake and Lizzie each put one foot on the ladder and hauled themselves up, shoving against the trapdoor together with their free hands, and managed to lift the grate enough to send the bigger rocks rolling off. Lizzie squirmed out through the opening, disappeared for a few moments, and then reappeared. "The area's secure."

It wasn't a trap at all.

"We're only a couple of miles from our extraction point," Lizzie said. "Let's seal up this grate so no-one can follow us, then see what we've got."

Filby tied down the trapdoor with a thin length of chain he drew from his bag, and they heaped the grate with rocks, ending up with a mound about two feet high. Nobody would be able to lift that from underneath.

"Hey, there they are," said Lizzie, pointing into the distance. A series of trucks drove through the desert, pulling up clouds of dust behind them. Filby reached into his bag and found his pair of binoculars. He watched for a few seconds, until one of the trucks screeched to a halt.

"Yes!" Filby said under his breath. Jake could tell something was going on. Filby passed his binoculars over, and Jake looked. He could see people running around madly, and one man running away from the trucks.

"You did it!" All three of them cheered, as they took turns watching the bombs explode and bees attacking each other.

Filby cracked his knuckles. "Okay, Hale. Let's see what's in the doctor's bag."

"I hope it's his diary," said Lizzie. "I love reading other peoples' diaries."

Jake opened the duffel bag and began lifting out the contents while Lizzie did a verbal inventory. "Two pairs boxer shorts, plaid. Ew. Four pairs socks, black. Who needs more socks than they need underwear? One sweatshirt, black. One pair of pants, black. Um, Hale, are you sure he said the bag was important? One toiletry bag — open that up, Filby. One toothbrush, some toothpaste, some dental floss, some razors. No secret pockets or compartments? Hmm."

"I think he just handed you his overnight bag, Hale," Filby said. "Too bad. We could have used some intel."

"Well, I also—" Jake began.

"Hey, there's something else in here," Lizzie said, taking the duffel bag from Jake's hands. She reached inside and drew out a heavy paperback book. "One well-thumbed copy of *War and Peace*. A little light reading, anyone? Wow, this book is heavier than a brick."

"If this bag was important, it could be the book," Filby said.

"Are you thinking what I'm thinking," asked Lizzie.

"A book code," said Filby.

"What's a book code?" Jake asked.

"It's a code, dumbass," said Lizzie, sarcastically. Jake glared at her.

"It's one of the classic code techniques," said Filby, as he flipped through the novel looking for clues. "You encode messages by writing where the words appear in any book. So if you want to use this word, you'd write 312-15-6. That means the word from page three hundred and twelve, on line fifteen, six words across. So as long as no one else knows what book you're using, the code is unbreakable. But maybe you've just found his code book!" He grinned.

"Or maybe this doctor guy just likes..." She glanced at the cover, and read the author's name. "Leo Toasty."

"I think you mean Tolstoy," laughed Filby. "Well, even if it is for a book code, it's not much good without secret messages." He sighed.

"Secret messages like these?" Jake handed over his HyperOpticon. "I found pages of codes in Doctor Eyebrows' office." Filby looked down and gaped at the pictures.

"This is amazing!"

"Hale!" Lizzie said, peering at the screen. "Why didn't you tell us you'd gotten this?"

"I tried," he began, but Filby shushed him again, reading over the pages that were written in clear text.

"This is interesting," Filby said. "Very interesting. There's not a lot of context, but something is supposed to happen on a train in Russia... the day after tomorrow." He looked up.

Filby connected the HyperOpticon to his Stormpad and began downloading the images, then pulled them up to full-screen size. Lizzie added the images to her Stormpad, too. She squinted at one of the pages crowded with numbers, then referred to the paperback book in her hands. "Oh, jeez. If this is the code, it's done with letters, not words. Let's see, first letter would be... 'o.'" She flipped through the book. "Next letter would be... 'p'..." She flipped back several pages. "Then 'e'..." She sighed. "This is going to take forever." After another minute, she smacked Jake on the shoulder. "Good job, new kid! The first word is 'Operation'! Unless this code is talking about an operation to get the Doctor's eyebrows thinned out, you might have uncovered some good intelligence here."

"Let's get to the extraction point," Filby said. "I was really hoping for a few days of sleep, but something tells me we might be heading to Russia."

"And you might be doing a little decoding," said Lizzie, handing Filby the heavy book while looking at him in a very bored way.

MEETING THE DOCTOR

The extraction point was a lonely plateau nestled among rocky hills, and a dirty white helicopter buzzed down at exactly seven minutes past the hour, as arranged — it was scheduled to check the site every two hours for the rest of the day. The helicopter flew them back to the tiny airstrip where they'd first landed in the Starbuster. Lizzie and Jake took advantage of the little metal cots in the office to get some sleep while Filby coordinated with Jenny on the next stage of their mission.

When Jake woke up, night had fallen outside, and Filby was munching a VindiqoQo and decoding the secret messages. He passed a candy bar over to Jake, and flipped to a new page. "309. 10. 12. 4. I bet Argentinian food is delicious," he said. "It's a shame we won't get to try any. Not even the Argentinian honey. By the way, be careful. That's Vindiqo fuel you're about to eat."

Jake stifled a yawn, shrugged, and took a bite of the bar — overly sugary, and it was delicious. "Guess you've joined the enemy," Filby laughed.

"Hm. How's the decoding going?"

"I'm up to Nizhny Novgorod."

"What?"

"I think you mean 'where.' It's the fifth-largest city in Russia. At least I hope so. I'm getting blisters on my fingers from breaking this code. But it looks like we have a train to catch. The Trans-Siberian."

Jake nodded, and wiped some sleep from his eyes. "The train from the Doctor's papers? It's in Russia?"

"It runs the whole way from Moscow to Vladivostok. Six thousand miles. Those train tracks cover twice the width of America."

"But why are we the ones going," Jake asked.

"We're the only ones that have seen the bees and the people behind it. They need our eyes and our analysis. But again, it's just recon."

"This trip was just supposed to be recon, too!"

Lizzie opened her eyes and exclaimed, "And look how much fun it turned out to be!"

"This is fun?" Jake said, as he massaged his bruised limbs.

A fist pounded against the door.

"Come on," Filby said. "They're ready. We've got a seventeen-hour plane trip ahead of us, and I've got about seventeen hours of decoding left to do. But don't worry, they're sending a more senior agent with us this time."

The plane was another business jet, but an older, less luxurious one, all ugly shades of brown inside, with no flat screen TVs. Jake almost laughed when he realized he was disappointed — he'd gotten used to flying around in private jets awfully quickly. Filby sank into a seat with his Stormpad propped against his knees, earbuds tucked in, off in his own world as he transcribed.

Jake took his seat, put in his own headphones, and woke up his Stormpad.

"Welcome back, agent Hale," Storm said.

"Hi Storm. Um, can I do a search for criminal suspects," he asked.

"Permission granted."

"I'm looking for a doctor."

"8,747,790 suspects found."

"Wow, that's a lot. He's a man. Does that narrow it down?"

"4,812,532 suspects found."

"Okay, let's see... he's about five feet ten, and medium build — maybe a little bit fat — he's white, and he's between forty and sixty years old."

"914,177 suspects found."

"We're getting somewhere I guess. He's got really blue eyes."

"20,976 suspects found."

"He wears glasses with round rims, he's got white hair, and... yeah, he has really bushy eyebrows."

"Twenty three suspects found."

"Now you're talking. Can I see pictures of the twenty three doctors?"

"Downloading imagery now."

Jake quickly flipped through the twenty three blue-eyed, chubby white doctors with bushy eyebrows and glasses — *no, no, not him, no way, definitely not, no, no, no* — and then stopped. The image practically jumped out of the Stormpad. There, staring back at him, was

Doctor Eyebrows. He was clean, combed, shaved (even the eyebrows, it looked like), and dressed in a well-fitting suit under a white medical coat. But it was definitely the angry man from the laboratory.

"Lizzie, come over here!"

She removed her earbuds and rushed over.

"Doctor Richard Horst," he read quietly as he touched the image. "This is the guy I saw in the lab, the guy with the duffel bag. This is Doctor Eyebrows."

"This is the guy with more socks than underwear?" she said. "I don't recognize him."

"Storm, can you tell us more about him?"

"Accessing case file."

After a pause, a video loaded, and a woman's voice began narrating over a photo of Doctor Eyebrows.

"Meet Doctor Richard Horst. Age 47. Born in South Africa, raised in England, trained at Oxford and then Harvard, he was the world's leading expert in genetic engineering. The medical world and the media hailed him as a genius ahead of his time, predicting he would lead globally-changing scientific breakthroughs in his lifetime, and awarded him 18 humanitarian awards in one short decade of medical service. He developed medicines, cured diseases, and saved lives."

"Are you sure this is the right guy," Lizzie said.

"Hold on," Jake said.

"However, this promising phase ended when former colleagues began making complaints. Hearings followed, as well an in-depth investigation, and

Doctor Horst was eventually stripped of every one of his licenses and certifications. All but one of his awards was taken away."

"Okay," Lizzie said. "Maybe this is your guy. Hey Stormy, what was he doing?"

"Doctor Horst was conducting illegal experiments on Burmese and North Korean political prisoners, injecting them with experimental medicines. When he exhausted his supply of sick prisoners, he infected healthy prisoners with diseases, allowed the diseases to take root, and then attempted to cure them. He killed thousands of prisoners a year."

"Whoa…" Lizzie said, stuttering a little. "That's… I didn't realize… That's just really bad."

"Doctor Horst has now been banned from practicing science or medicine across the globe," the computer said, "but he continues to operate illegally. Twice more he has been convicted, in absentia, of conducting illegal experiments on human test subjects."

"What are the new experiments he's been doing?" Jake asked.

"Specific details are unknown, but all subjects died excruciating, painful deaths from the operations."

"That's just sick," said Lizzie, her face contorted in disgust.

"Doctor Horst has since moved underground, and his current whereabouts are unknown. Unconfirmed rumors maintain that he is now connected with Vindiqo."

"Yeah," said Jake. "In Argentina. And I think we can call those rumors confirmed now, Storm. We saw him. So what's the one award that didn't get taken away?"

"Conscientious Medical Champion of the Year."

Jake and Lizzie looked at each other, confused.

"Who gave it to him?" she asked.

"Vindiqo Products and Resources Corporation," the voice of the Stormpad responded.

Jake played around with the Stormpad for several hours, doing more research on bees and Vindiqo. After checking to make sure the time zones lined up right, he got Jenny to patch him through to his parents, to let him know he was doing okay. "How's the spy game?" his dad asked.

"I'm heading to Russia. Things got messed up in Argentina — I was just supposed to do recon, but I had to invade a terrorist base to rescue my friends," Jake said, knowing it was pointless. "They'd been kidnapped."

"Argentina, eh?" his mom said. "That's exciting, but Russia is so much more traditional spy territory. The KGB, Red Square, Lenin's mausoleum… oh the good old days."

Jake laughed. "Yeah, Filby said pretty much the same thing."

They said their farewells, and Jake felt an icy stab of homesickness right in his chest. Being a secret agent was definitely exciting, but there was something to be said for his own town, his own house, his own bed. Thinking of bed made him remember the dictum to "sleep when you can," so he reclined his chair and closed his eyes.

He woke up when the plane touched down on a runway, and blinked around, trying to remember where he was and what he was supposed to be doing. Filby was eating a bagel, and Lizzie emerged from the little bedroom, scratching her head.

"It's about seven at night here," Filby said, munching away. "We've got time to grab some dinner — or breakfast — before we get on the train."

"We're in Russia?" Jake peered out the window. They appeared to be at a commercial airport, judging by the big jets on the runways and all the trucks and baggage handlers rushing around.

"Kirov," Filby said. "The Trans-Siberian railway comes right through here. From the codes you found, we know something is happening near Nizhny Novgorod, on the train. That's still a few hundred miles away, so we have time to work it out. You ever been on a train, Hale?"

"Sure, a couple of times."

Filby nodded. "I haven't. One of my foster parents had a train set in the basement, but we weren't allowed to touch it. They've annoyed me ever since."

"Foster parents?" Jake asked, as Lizzie interrupted saying, "I've always wanted to have a fight on top of a moving train! How awesome would that be?"

"It's not as awesome as you think," a man said as he climbed on board. "You get a lot of smoke in your eyes, and it's incredibly windy. Stick to fighting inside the train — that's my advice. Hello, agents."

It was Snakesman!

TRANS-SIBERIAN

"The documents you sent us imply a senior underground member of Vindiqo will be on the train," said Snakesman. "He's someone I'd like to talk to, so while the three of you are trying to solve this bee riddle, I'll track him down. If it's who I think it is, he could be extremely useful. Now, here's your cover: you're American cousins." He handed out incredibly believable passports to each of the agents. Lizzie and Filby automatically flipped them open and started reading to themselves. "Names and dates and addresses are in there. Memorize them."

Jake looked at his new passport, and was surprised to see a picture of himself he never remembered being taken, alongside the name "Nathan Hale Kipling."

"I'm your uncle, showing you my birthplace, which is Nizhny Novgorod. My cover name is Alexander Morozov, but you may call me Uncle Sasha." He pointed to Lizzie and shot out, "Who are you?"

She didn't hesitate. "Kari Goodsill. I'm 13, from Chicago, I go to Middlebrook High." Snakesman pointed to Filby.

"I'm Stanley Lamp, from LA. I'm 14."

"Which part of LA, Stanley?"

"Pasadena."

Snakesman now pointed to Jake, and Jake's mind went absolutely blank.

"Something Hale... something," he stuttered out.

"You are no longer a new kid, Hale. You must learn your cover. Three people your age boarding the Trans-Siberian won't attract attention, but your use of English will. You're Nathan Hale Kipling. Why are you getting on the train, Nathan Hale Kipling?"

"Um... to see my uncle Sasha's hometown."

"Which is?"

"Nizhny Nov- Nizhny Novgorod!"

"Excellent. Learn your cover. Now, tactical matters will be up to you three. Keep an eye out for anything strange. What is the connection between Argentina and this train? What is the plan for these bees? They no longer seem to be quite the miracle bees the first reports implied. We have a private sleeper car to use as a base of operations."

"The bees in Argentina," Jake said to Snakesman, "They were loaded with poison."

"I know, Hale, and good work. Filby put that in his report. Speaking of which, Lizzie, why didn't you submit a report?" He scowled, but she just looked away innocently until he passed out small plastic pairs of handcuffs.

"These are extremely strong," Snakesman said. "Just in case."

A big smile came over Lizzie's face.

Once they all had their gear together, they took the stairs down directly to the runway. The night air was warm and pleasant. "Huh," Jake said. "I thought Russia would be full of snow, ice, and fur hats..."

"Dancing Cossacks drinking vodka?" Lizzie said. "Grizzly bears wandering the streets?"

Jake shrugged. "What do I know?"

They followed Snakesman into the airport, where he had a conversation in rapid Russian with an official. Jake got the sense the two men had some kind of prior arrangement, since there was a lot of smiling and handshaking. The official glanced briefly at their passports, then unzipped their bags — all the gear was put away in hidden pockets or concealed underneath clothing — for a quick check. Then he smiled, handed the bags back, and told them to "Enjoy your stay" in perfect English.

The airport was grayer and dingier than the ones Jake was used to in the US, and there were more men wandering around with machine guns, but it still wasn't much like the spy movies about Russia he'd seen with his dad.

"It wasn't always so easy to walk around here," Snakesman said. "Not so many years ago, this would have been unthinkable — four Westerners just strolling through. But now they're just happy to have tourists. That's progress, isn't it? The world can become a better place."

Out on the curb, a battered brown station wagon was waiting, driven by a man with thinning, slicked-back hair and an ugly flowered shirt. Snakesman spoke to him in Russian, and they stowed their bags in the back. The driver gestured for them to get in, then got behind the wheel.

"There are no seatbelts," Jake said.

Lizzie, sitting in the backseat between Jake and Filby, grinned. "Don't worry. I'm sure you'll soon be doing stuff a lot more dangerous than riding in a station wagon death trap."

As far as he could tell in the dark, Kirov was a city like any other: buildings, buses, apartment houses, shops (at least the signs were in Russian), scraggly urban trees, dirty cars. He brightened when they passed a church with the tall, onion-shaped towers he imagined when he thought about Russia. Soon they drove over a long, beautiful, multi-arched bridge, spanning a vast river.

Not long after crossing the river they reached the train station, a big grayish-white building with a triangular roof. Snakesman paid the driver and led the team into the crowded station.

The platform was covered with people hawking Russian nesting dolls, scarves, jewelry, and food, and vendors grilling meat on open fires right there in the open, just steps from the tracks. It had the atmosphere of a flea market or a street festival, and Jake thought the average American Amtrak station could benefit from some guys grilling kebabs next to the ticket booth.

Although it was extremely discreet, Jake noticed that Snakesman's eyes never stopped moving. He glanced at every person they passed, no doubt using his skills at reading body language to scout out potential threats. He beckoned the group close and spoke in a low voice. "I am now quite sure that there will be Vindiqo employees on the train. I don't know how many, or who, but I already recognize one man."

Jake did his best not to turn around.

"He is dressed as a train employee, pushing that trolley loaded with large steamer trunks."

The station platform was far too loud and busy for Jake and the others to hear, but up close the steamer trunks were quietly buzzing.

RIDING THE RAILS

They approached one of the train doors, where a uniformed conductor looked over their tickets, then directed them to board the train. They went down a narrow hallway with windows on one side and sliding wooden doors on the other, each door numbered. "This is ours," Snakesman said, sliding open one of the doors and ducking his head inside to look around before gesturing that they should enter.

The sleeper car was small, with two bench seats that doubled as beds, covered in blue blankets. Higher on the walls were two other beds, folded up against the walls for now. There was also a little table, recessed drawers, and even a real glass vase holding flowers.

Jake picked up the vase, and laughed. "Russians really know how to make a train ride feel fancy," he said.

"If only the beds were more comfortable," Filby said, sitting on one and bouncing up and down. "Fortunately, we won't be sleeping much."

"So what do we do if we find something?" Jake asked.

"The extraction point is marked on your Stormpads," said Snakesman. "If I'm on the train, find me. If I've already left, make your own way there.

There'll be a pickup attempt twice a day for the next five days. And if there's anything you need to leave for me..." He slid open a small compartment hidden under the bottom bunk. "Dead drop it."

"I'm going to take a walk around," Lizzie said. "Keep an eye out for bad guys, okay?"

With a wink, she was gone.

Snakesman waved as he wandered off in the opposite direction, and Filby stood and stretched. "I'm going with Snakesman," he said, tossing Jake the copy of *War and Peace,* and his decoded transcript.

"I'm getting sick of Tolstoy," he said. "Maybe you can finish it?" And then he was gone. The train jerked forward, then began to smoothly accelerate. Jake watched the other trains at the depot disappear on both sides, seeming to slide backward and away.

"I guess it's just you and me," he said to the book, as he started to review Filby's scrawled deciphered notes.

"Operation on schedule," they began. "Trans-Siberia Express, westward bound, project will require multiple unloads time releases according to original schedule with additional releases in section 7 and 8 and 15..." He started to yawn. The text was dry enough and vague enough that it meant absolutely nothing to him. The lack of punctuation — Filby had guessed here and there — made it even worse. He skimmed to the end, and it was just as bad:

"Once this mission has been completed the hive colonies across the U.K. (?) Raine will meet with certain..."

Jake groaned when he read those initials: the United Kingdom, England. Maybe they were in the wrong place, and would have to fly back there in a few hours. He looked at the next page reference. 389-9-3. At least it was a full word instead of just letters. He stifled another yawn, and turned to page 389. He counted down towards the ninth line, but he didn't really have to count. He didn't have to count three words across, either. One word practically jumped off the page: "Death."

The hive colonies across the U.K. (?) Raine will meet with certain death.

But this meant nothing. Who was Raine? He counted the words again. Death was definitely the ninth line, the third word. He checked the page number, 389. Outside the window, Russian countryside flew past. He thought about different ways to phrase it... maybe whoever had coded this had made a mistake?

The hive colonies across the U.K. (?) Raine will meet with certain death.

He ran to the door and opened it, looking down the train's wobbling corridor. Two shabby, unshaven men leaned out a window, smoking foul cigarettes and laughing. A fat woman in a dark blue military uniform pushed her way through. But there was no Filby, and no Lizzie, and no Snakesman in sight.

"Ugh," cursed Jake to himself, as he slammed the door and picked up the book again. 425-17-12-1. He turned to the four hundred and twenty-fifth page, and looked down seventeen lines, and wrote down the first letter of the twelfth word. It was "t." Working slowly, his fingers drying out from the endless flipping of pages, he managed to spell out "The aviary will be kept in carriage..."

As letters, they meant nothing, but reading the sentence Jake started to tremble. "The aviary..." He remembered that was another name for a beehive. The bees... "In carriage..." Surely this meant on the train... The bees were on the train! He raced to decode the crucial next letters — it felt like it took hours to decode the single word "three" — then pulled out his ticket, searching for a carriage number. The ticket was in Russian, but it looked like it said he was in carriage fourteen. The bees were at the other end of the train!

Jake ran from the compartment and into the passageway, bringing his backpack with him. The two men were still there, smoking and talking loudly.

"V chem delo?" one of them asked abruptly.

"Huh?"

"Why you run, boy?" he said in broken English. "Where is the fire?" The other man laughed as Jake smiled his way past them. *That's right — keep your cool, maintain your cover*, he thought.

He strolled along, trying to look like he just wanted to tour the train while his head was racing inside. He turned to glance into the sleeper cars that had open doors, nodding and smiling at the old women, businessmen, and scowling mothers who occupied them, wondering if any of them worked for Vindiqo.

Where are Filby and Lizzie, he thought. *How do I always get stranded like this?*

Jake reached the end of the car and puzzled for a moment over how to open the door there, and almost pushed a large red button before realizing it wasn't the door opener, it was the emergency brake signal. He exhaled, grateful he hadn't blown his cover with something as stupid as that, remembering that he'd seen them scattered along the length of the train. *Focus, Jake, focus*, he thought, as he realized that he had to twist a metal bar to open the door. He passed between the train cars, noticing the rubber sleeve that surrounded the gap between cars. That made sense, though it would make Lizzie's dream of fighting on the rooftop that much harder to achieve.

The next car held more sleeper compartments, though most of them were open and empty.

The one after was crowded though, rows and rows of seats jammed with people holding luggage on their laps, bouncing babies on legs, slurping from cups of noodles, sipping from thermoses, and reading newspapers covered in Russian letters that he couldn't read. None of them were Lizzie or Filby.

He saw two boys with blonde hair shoving each other in adjacent seats and had a heart-stopping moment when he thought they were the twins, but they were too young.

Jake pushed through to the next car, a lounge filled with men playing cards and chess. But no Stormglass faces here either. Where were they? He picked up speed as he walked through that crowd, then into the dining car. There were tablecloths, red and gold decorations on the walls, even potted plants, and waiters pouring drinks and carrying plates. One of the waiters spoke to him in Russian, then in English when Russian got no response: "You want eat food?"

"Uh, no, thanks, just looking around," Jake said, but the waiter was already shooing him out of the way. Jake hurried through the car to the far door, and opened it to carriage seven. He was worried that he wouldn't find the others before he reached carriage three — *what happened to them?* Nervous and distracted, Jake bumped into a man in a conductor's uniform.

"Oh, sorry," Jake said. "I didn't mean to—"

A gloved hand clamped down on his shoulder, and he looked up. Gray eyes, a dangerous smile, and a long white scar stared back at him. The hand squeezed, so hard that Jake almost screamed from the pain.

"Well, well," the man said calmly. "If it isn't the new boy. Well, we meet again. It's Hale, right? See, now I know your name."

TERROR AND INTERROGATION

"And I know yours," Jake said. "Mundt."

The man narrowed his eyes and bared his teeth. "Aren't we friendly now? Come along, little boy."

Jake started to twist away, but Mundt clamped down harder, and Jake whimpered and went still. The pain was so great, he thought he might black out.

"I don't have a gun today," Mundt said, "but I can do a lot of damage without one. I could crush the bones in your shoulder to splinters without even trying."

Jake thought about his Aikido lessons. Maybe he could hurt the man, maybe even injure him and escape, crazy bionic arm or not — but then Mundt squeezed again, and Jake's vision swam with black spots.

Mundt pushed Jake through to the mostly-empty sleeper car, and shoved him into the nearest vacant compartment, 723. Jake fell to the bed, and looked around — this was an exact duplicate of his compartment, even with the vase of flowers. Mundt stepped in and slid the door shut behind him.

"I assume your little friends are here as well, lurking around," Mundt said, looming over Jake. "But who else is here? And what did you uncover in Argentina?"

"Did all the bees die?" Jake said. "When the bombs went off in the back of the trucks?"

Mundt's lips compressed into a thin line, and he opened and closed his hands like he wanted to strangle someone. "I ask the questions here, boy."

"Actually, I do," said a muffled voice behind him as the door flew open.

The man swiveled, and Jake grabbed the vase to slam into Mundt's head. Mundt sensed the movement and turned back just in time for the vase to smash into his nose, making him reel backward and shout a curse as Filby plunged into the room and glass shattered to the floor. Jake tried to land a second blow, but Mundt twisted and swatted hard, slamming the iron prosthetic into his face and knocking him aside.

Filby raised a leg and kicked Mundt hard in the small of the back. Mundt reeled forward, stumbled into one of the bench seats, and without even thinking Jake jumped on his back, pushing down on the back of the Mundt's head until his face was buried in the fabric of the seat.

Filby snatched Mundt's wrist, snapping one of the handcuffs around it, and Jake helped wrench the other arm back so Filby could secure that one, too. Now Mundt was sprawled halfway across the bed, his wrists bound behind him, with Jake kneeling on his back. He strained against the cuffs, his face turning red, skin pulling against them. His faced even started to turn blue. Finally he grunted, and relaxed. Jake was surprised at how easy it was to tackle a Vindiqo henchman. Had the two days of training really been that good?

"So," Mundt panted. "You have me." He turned his face away from the thin blanket and cushion, and Jake noticed a circular scar on his temple — as if someone had cut a hole into his skull. "You're like dogs chasing cars, you know. What will you do now that you've caught me?"

Filby winked at Jake, drew a small metal flashlight from his pocket, and pressed the cold end against the back of Mundt's neck. The man with the scar hissed, but didn't move. "Do you feel that?" Filby said.

"You wouldn't shoot me," Mundt said. "Not with your silly little flashlight, at least."

Filby shrugged, removed the flashlight, took a step back, slid the door closed, and engaged the lock. Mundt snorted.

"How do you see this working out, little boy?"

"I ask the questions now," Filby said. "And you'll answer them."

Mundt laughed bitterly. "There is nothing you could offer or threaten to make me talk."

"I guess not," Filby said. "I'm nobody special. But the kid sitting on your back right now? You pulled a gun on him not so long ago. You were planning to do some very nasty things to him in this very room. Maybe you should worry about what he'll do to you, especially if you won't cooperate?"

"Ha," Mundt sneered. "Come here, little boy."

Filby moved closer.

"No, closer."

"I'd watch it, Filby," said Jake. "I mean, Stanley."

"Come closer, boy. I'll tell you something."

Filby moved even closer. And that's when Mundt lunged, grabbing a section of Filby's arm in his teeth. Filby cried out loud, punching at Mundt's face with his free hand. As Mundt twisted and shook, and Filby desperately tried to pull away, Jake frantically looked for something else to hit him with — a rock, a piece of broken glass, a stupid shoe? Suddenly, he remembered. He ran into the corridor, down the train, ignoring Filby's frantic cries.

Jake got halfway down the car before he found one of the red emergency break buttons, and slammed his hand against it as hard as he could. The train jerked and screeched and he heard a loud bang from the room. He ran back, and Mundt was out cold. The man had slammed his head into the wall. Filby was clenching his arm, trying to stop the pain from the bite wound.

"That man is a maniac," he said. "He better not have rabies. Look, I'm bleeding!"

"Here," Jake said as he ripped a piece of sheet into a tourniquet. "Wrap this around your arm."

Jake ripped another strip of sheet, and bundled it into Mundt's mouth, then went through his pockets. There was nothing.

"Thanks, Hale," Filby said, surveying the unconscious criminal.

"No worries," Jake said, catching his breath and feeling guilty for having suspected Filby as a traitor.

"Now we've only got one other problem. There are bees on the train."

The pair raced through the cars as the train picked up speed again, Filby hugging his arm, and both of them laughing to give the impression that they were just kids having fun. They kept an eye out for Lizzie and Snakesman and — most of all — for Doctor Horst, or any other Vindiqo thugs. It wasn't long before they reached carriage three, the carriage with the bees. The name of the car was written in both English and Russian. It said, "Luggage Car — Locked." And it was unlocked.

Jake took point through the door, going in low, with Filby following behind him. The car was full of sweet-smelling smoke, making the space a shadowy mess of trunks, bags, and crates. "Was Lizzie here?" Jake coughed.

"Still am," she called cheerily. "I'm in the back!"

Jake and Filby made their way to the back of the car, where Lizzie sat on a big metal drum that somehow looked familiar. "I encountered some resistance," she said, coughing and gesturing toward a pair of burly men sprawled unconscious on the floor. "But I found out what our mission should have been."

"Where are the bees?" Jake asked.

Lizzie lifted an eyebrow. "How did you know?"

"It was in the Tolstoy," Jake smiled.

She nodded, and kicked her foot out towards a large steamer trunk. "They're in there, and in eight other trunks just like it. They are not happy about the situation. They were buzzing louder than the engines of a biker gang. Actually, listen…"

All three waited quietly. There was only the sound of the train and the rocking metal drums scattered throughout the carriage.

"Yep. I think they all killed each other," she said.

"But why were the bees on the train?" asked Filby.

"Releases," said Jake, as he remembered the encoded message. "The code said they'd be releasing them, 'in section 7 and 8 and 15.' Those must be places. They were trying to kill someone named Raine."

"Who?" asked Lizzie.

"Raine," said Jake, as Filby nodded remembering. "The note said something about England — no, about the hive colonies across the UK — and that Raine would meet with certain death.'"

As Jake spoke the words out loud, he suddenly realized what the message actually meant. 'U.K.' wasn't about England, and 'Raine' wasn't a man. They were one word — Ukraine, the country that bordered Russia.

"Ukraine is the fifth largest producer of honey in the world," said Filby, realizing the same thing. "There are millions of beehives in the country — and tens of billions of honeybees. But 'certain death'? Why would the hives meet with certain death?"

All three remained silent, trying to work out the riddle.

"What do the bees do?" asked Filby. "They're saving the world, and what else?"

"They kill cats," Lizzie said.

"That still makes no sense," said Filby. "That must have just been a mistake."

"They attacked us," said Jake.

"That definitely wasn't a mistake," said Filby.

"Wait," Jake said suddenly. "What was it Jenny said? What did the bees do in the attack?"

"Well, in case you forgot, they almost killed us," said Lizzie.

"No, I mean, yes, but they also killed the Beekeeper's bees," said Jake. "What if these bees aren't just replacements for the dying bees? What if they're trained to kill other bees?"

"Bees trained to kill bees?" asked Lizzie, confused. And then she slapped her head as she understood. "Bees trained to kill bees! So that all the natural bees would be dead, and everyone would have to buy Vindiqo bees!"

"Yes! Why buy bees if you already have bees," said Filby, catching on. "Hale, you're right. If these bees took over in Ukraine, they'd spread throughout Europe and China. These bees could kill off all the natural honeybees in the world!"

"That's absolutely brilliant," said Lizzie. "Sick and deranged, but brilliant! That must have been where the trucks in Argentina were going — to release bees there, too! Vindiqo could hold the entire world hostage! If you want fruit and crops to grow, you have to buy Vindiqo bees!"

"We need to find Snakesman and let him know," said Filby.

"No, we need to get off this train," said Lizzie, hopping off the metal drum, "and soon! These guys knew I was from Stormglass, and I wouldn't be surprised if the next station is crawling with Vindiqo agents."

"What did you do to them anyway?" asked Jake, opening the heavy door.

Lizzie grinned. "I used that whole little-lost-girl routine — you know, 'Help, I went to the bathroom and now I can't find my mummy.' I spoke in very good Russian, with my high-class Muscovite accent."

"You speak Russian?" asked Jake, amazed, as they passed four men playing cards and drinking from bottles in paper bags.

"Yeah — I learned it for my first big case. But these guys didn't buy it for a second. It almost seemed like they were waiting for me. They actually pulled guns on me! I had a smoke grenade ready, so I rolled it in here and slammed the door shut again. When I opened it, they were out. Not cool, though."

"So how did they know we were coming?" he asked.

Filby turned around and frowned. "That doctor, what's his name, Horst? He must have realized we'd found his book and cracked the code. He must have warned them that we'd show up."

Jake was thinking of another explanation, and an explanation that seemed to make more and more sense: that Jenny was the traitor.

"They knew we were coming, that's all that matters," Lizzie said as they reached their carriage. "And pretty soon they'll know we were here."

"Where's Snakesman," Jake asked. The room was still empty.

"He can take care of himself," said Lizzie, grabbing her bag and whipping it open. "Let's get out of here."

"Let me just leave him a message," Jake said. He scrawled a note on a scrap of thick waxy Russian toilet paper, and slipped it into the hidden dead drop.

Lizzie had already booted up her Stormpad. "Three minutes until we reach a bend in the track. We'd better get ready."

"Ready for what?" Jake said.

"We're going to jump."

As the train wrapped around the bend, Jake and Filby hauled the window open, letting in a whipping rush of air. They were in the middle of nowhere, nothing around them but stands of white-barked trees and a hill up ahead with a tunnel punched through it.

"Go," shouted Lizzie, pushing Jake out the window. Filby jumped next, and then Lizzie came last. Each of them managed to stay upright, and pelted into the forest.

"Now we move," Lizzie said. "We've got to put a lot of distance between us and this train."

"No welbikes this time, huh?" Jake said.

"Nope," Filby said unhappily. "The most advanced transportation technology we've got this time is our own feet."

"At least until somebody invents welfeet," Lizzie laughed.

As they started walking, Filby turned to Jake. "So what did you leave for Snakesman?"

"I told him our dead drop package was too big to fit in the box, so we left it in room 723."

"That's where we left Mundt?" Filby asked. Jake nodded, and they both started laughing.

THE FINAL MISSION

"Does anyone live out here?"

They picked their way through the sparse forest of tall, almost unnaturally straight trees. Fortunately the trees were pale — they almost glowed in the moonlight, which made it easier to avoid bumping into them. They'd been walking for hours, over fields and through trees, following Lizzie and her uncanny sense of direction. Jake was hungry, and his feet hurt, and the powerful thrill of capturing Mundt had faded, though it was still a pleasant memory.

"There are small towns a few miles away in pretty much any direction," Lizzie said, "but there's nothing here — that's why it makes a great extraction point." They emerged from the latest stand of trees, and Lizzie pointed. "There, that shack is the meeting place."

A half-collapsed wooden house — no bigger than a garage — stood surrounded by trees. There were no signs of life, but Lizzie crept around and peered in the windows before signaling that Jake and Filby should approach and enter.

Snakesman was waiting inside the shack — with Mundt. He was still handcuffed, and gagged, and sitting on the one rickety wooden chair in the dim space. The man glared at Jake with narrow, dark eyes.

Jake had the bizarre urge to apologize — but the guy had pulled a gun on him.

"I found your note," Snakesman said, with a smile. "Nice touch."

"How did you beat us here?" Jake said.

"I drenched him in vodka, pretended he was drunk, and walked him off the train. Disgraceful, really. A local farmer drove us out here in exchange for a few rubles. And that's that."

"Where were you?" asked Jake.

Snakesman laughed, embarrassed. "Would you believe in the toilet? I don't understand how the three of you managed to cause so much trouble in so little time. But we're all here now. Two transports will be along soon. One will escort Mundt and myself back to Stormglass headquarters, and the other is for you."

"What's going to happen to him?" Jake said.

"He'll face justice for his crimes."

"I think I know what the bees are doing," said Jake. Snakesman lifted one eyebrow curiously. "I don't think they're trying to save the world at all. Or if they are, that's just part of it. I think the bees were really manufactured to cause colony collapse disorder!"

Snakesman frowned, and pulled the gag from Mundt's mouth. "Is this the truth, Igor?"

Mundt gave Snakesman a murderous glare.

"I wouldn't tell you anything, backstabber. I want my lawyer."

Mundt shoved the gag back in his mouth.

"You'll get a lawyer, don't worry about that."

"So evidently you get to go back to headquarters," Lizzie said. "Where are we going?"

"East Africa," Snakesman said. Mundt winced and looked away. "Specifically, Tanzania. We've been processing data from the computers recovered in Argentina, and it looks like Budapest is the main headquarters — we're sending senior agents there — but Tanzania appears to have a secondary, smaller base. And I know Jenny told you the same thing before, but this mission we're serious: this is only for intel gathering. Whatever you do, don't even think about entering the base, okay? And don't let yourselves be caught this time! That seems to be the only way you end up in these messes."

All three agents looked down abashed, holding back their smirks of accomplishment. Yes, they'd messed up a bit, but they'd also cracked this case wide open.

"By the way, Jenny won't be helping out on this mission any more."

Jake looked up, eyes wide. *Jenny was the traitor!* "Why," he asked urgently.

"The reason is operationally irrelevant," Snakesman said. "I'll coordinate with you while I'm in the air."

An engine rumbled outside. Snakesman looked out through a crack between two boards nailed over the window frame. "That's your ride, agents. You'll be taken to an airfield and flown to Tanzania. We haven't had time to arrange a grand welcome, so you'll be going in with the gear you have on hand.

And just in case something does go wrong... Do you still have any pheromone bombs?"

"A few," Lizzie said. "Maybe not enough for a million bees though."

"Fire is also good for killing bees," Snakesman said, "and you know how to make fire, Lizzie. Burn something from the inside?"

"I do indeed," she said, with a strange smile on her face.

"But only as a last resort. I'll be in touch through your Stormpads, and I'll send you details on extraction while you're en route to Tanzania. And remember: you've only got two goals, and they're broad, and simple. Watch, and report."

"What if they get away?" Filby said.

"If you don't start moving, they will. Get going!"

The gray-haired, gaunt driver of the rusty blue sedan waiting outside didn't even look at them when they piled inside with their bags. He drove silently down dark roads for long enough that Jake began to doze off, until the car abruptly halted. Jake peered blearily out the window. They were outside a low-slung building with a metal roof, presumably at another tiny airfield.

Jake couldn't recall how many airfields he'd seen in the past few days. Everything was starting to run together, and if not for the occasional burst of adrenaline, he wasn't sure he'd even be able to stand upright. He needed food and sleep and rest. What if he missed something important, some vital clue? He'd been recruited because he was observant, but he was having trouble even observing the contents of his own mind.

Lizzie said something to the driver in Russian — a question, it sounded like — and he barked a response. "We're here," she translated. They climbed out of the car, and were met by another Russian operative, this one in his teens, who rushed them toward a gleaming, low-slung jet. As he did so, Jake noticed he made a subtle "S" with his hands. He was another agent. Lizzie whistled and spoke to their guide, then laughed. "This is a nice plane, guys. I've ridden in it before! Come on."

They tromped up the steps into the interior, and Jake looked around, dazzled. The inside of the plane was like an explosion in a jewelry box. Everything was gleaming gold and encrusted with what had to be fake jewels — because who would put actual rubies and sapphires on the armrest of a chair? The curtains in the windows were thick red velvet with gold accents, and the seats were white leather. An actual chandelier dangled from the ceiling. They all prowled around the interior, opening cabinets and looking in cupboards. Jake went to investigate the bathroom, where the fixtures were all gold. The private cabin in the rear had a waterbed — and a hot tub, though that was empty.

Jake went dazedly back to the main cabin, where Lizzie and Filby were sprawled on one of the couches. "Guys. There's a waterbed back there. And a hot tub."

Lizzie snorted. "This plane belonged to some rich Russian, a guy who owned a million oil companies. He gave it to Stormglass. Not sure why, but at last we're traveling in style."

Jake found a deep armchair across from their couch and sank down into it. "So how long until we get to Tanzania?"

"Nine or ten hours," Filby said. "Just enough time to get an actual night's sleep."

"Perfect," Jake said, exhausted.

"Dibs on the waterbed," Lizzie shouted, as she headed towards the bathroom at the back.

THE TRAITOR (3)

The traitor made sure the bathroom door was shut securely, then made the call. The Doctor's face appeared on the smartphone screen, looking tired.

"Update me, my friend," the Doctor said in a soft voice.

"The next stop is Tanzania."

"Perfect. They took the bait, then. And what's happening to our good friend, Mundt?"

"I'm sorry — they caught him. It really wasn't my fault. He's being delivered to the Stormglass headquarters."

"Oh, outstanding," the Doctor said. "You did perfectly, everything is working exactly as I'd hoped. It'll all be over in a day or two, and then both of us can relax. Relax with the riches we've earned — the riches you've earned us! Yes, my little Stormglass agent, everything is fitting together so absolutely perfectly."

"But Doctor, what's going happen to the others? When we get to Tanzania? They don't realize the true story about Stormglass. They're actually good people."

"Why, if they're good people, I'll give them a choice," the Doctor said, the kindness in his voice sounding almost entirely sincere. "I'm a great believer in choices."

INTO THE JUNGLE

After the long plane flight, they landed at a dusty, remote airstrip. From there they rode in the back of a truck, hidden under empty burlap sacks, bumping along rough roads for what felt like hours. Their driver, a Tanzanian woman in a military-looking camouflage outfit, finally dropped them off on the side of a dirt track that cut through dense jungle.

The three of them promptly set off into the vine-wrapped trees, Jake and Filby following Lizzie's lead. Before they'd gone too far, she brought out a can of insect repellant and sprayed her neck and hands.

"What's that for?" Jake asked. "They have bad mosquitoes here?"

"Tsetse flies," Lizzie said. "They carry sleeping sickness. You don't want to catch that."

As they slathered on bug spray, Filby said, "What we really need is leopard spray. Because of the leopards." When they didn't laugh, he added, "Since they'll try to eat us." He paused. "There are snakes, too."

"That's reassuring," Jake said, nervously glancing around.

They spent two hours hiking through the jungle, heading west toward the coast. The temperature was bearable under the shade, an endlessly thick canopy of tree branches, but the humidity was insane. Jake couldn't tell if he was more sticky from the combination of sweat and bug spray or from the moisture in the air.

They did see plenty of snakes, which mostly slithered away when the trio approached. There were also spiders, weird birds, and monkeys, but fortunately no leopards — at least none they could see.

"Maybe it's the leopards we can't see that we need to worry about," Jake whispered to himself, stepping over a branch.

Lizzie consulted her Stormpad a few times on the trek, altering their course as they crossed over fallen trees furry with rot and moss and fungus, and tried to find places to ford creeks that were almost wide enough to qualify as rivers. Eventually they crested a ridge and discovered a breathtaking view: rocks tumbling down to an empty white sand beach, palm trees, and endless vistas of blue water beyond.

"Okay, I think we're a little bit lost," said Lizzie, ignoring the landscape and studying her Stormpad. "Maybe we should have taken a left at the overgrown tree with the mud pit." Jake and Filby both groaned.

"The northern coast of Tanzania is a lot more tourist-friendly," Filby said, taking out binoculars and peering through them at the beaches below. "This far south, there aren't any big cities, and not many people around, just occasional villages. It's discreet."

"The perfect place for a secret killer bee lab," said Jake as he sat on a rock, took a long drink of water, and wiped sweat from his forehead. "I can't believe how hot it is. We should have come in the winter."

"It's not any different then," Filby said, still scanning the beach below. "The only seasons here are 'wet' and 'dry'."

"Is this wet?"

"Nope. This is dry. The nicest time of year to be here. If it was wet, the sky would be dumping buckets of rain on us. Endlessly."

Jake groaned. "I wish we could go for a swim in the water down there." He glanced at Filby. "Let me guess. It's full of sharks?"

Filby shrugged.

"The base is definitely nearby," Lizzie said, frustrated. "If we make our way north, I think we'll-"

"Footprints," Jake exclaimed under his breath. Twenty feet away, fresh footprints led through the jungle. They were large, like an adult's.

"Someone's near here," whispered Lizzie. "Maybe someone from Vindiqo."

All three froze while they listened, but all they could hear was jungle noise.

"Be extra-quiet," Filby suggested. "Just to be safe."

They set off again, following close to the trail of prints and staying low, hidden by the trees. After fifteen or twenty minutes of silent, careful movement, Jake noticed a thin line glimmering in the light. He grabbed Lizzie firmly by her backpack, and held her from touching it.

"Tripwire," he whispered, pointing.

She ducked down and squinted, and saw a thin wire running at ankle height between two trees. Clearly someone had planned for unexpected visitors to approach this way. Lizzie examined the wire, tracing it to the point where it disappeared into the ground.

"It could be wired," she said quietly.

"The wire could be wired? To do what?" asked Jake, feeling slightly foolish even though he'd just saved her from tripping on it.

"Explosives, an alarm, drop a big spiked log on top us. We'll go around. Step where I step. Hale, keep your eagle eyes working." She slowly set off on a looping path, through deeper vegetation, moving aside fronds and vines gently with a stick as she went, looking for traps.

Jake followed, Filby behind him, puffing a little from the exertion. Lizzie stopped again, and used her stick to reveal a pit, eight-feet deep and covered with leaves and vines. "No spikes at the bottom," she whispered. "I guess that means they want to take visitors alive. I can't decide if that's reassuring or not."

Looking down, Jake wasn't so sure how welcoming that pit would be. He pictured breaking both legs in the fall.

They pressed on, and soon Lizzie held up a hand, signaling halt. She mouthed one word: "There." Filby and Jake carefully and quietly opened their folding binoculars to take a look.

There were several structures hidden among the trees, which had only been partially cleared, presumably so the foliage would hide the facility from planes and satellites. The buildings had cinderblock walls with metal roofs that were rusting in the moist air. Behind the buildings Jake glimpsed the rotors of a helicopter. While they watched, a bored-looking guard sauntered past, an assault weapon slung casually over his shoulder, walking the perimeter.

"Okay," Lizzie said in the quietest of whispers. "Let's split up. Filby, see if you can work your way around that way. Hale, you stick with me. We'll rendezvous on the other side."

"If I'm going alone," Filby whispered, "can you give me the tranquilizer gun? I don't have as much practice knocking out armed men as you."

Lizzie nodded, opened her pack and removed the bulky black pistol. "It's got five darts left. If you have to use it, be sure to hide any guards. We don't want to raise the alarm." She turned back to peer at the facility.

"Sure," Filby said as he pointed the gun at Lizzie and pulled the trigger.

BETRAYAL

Jake gasped, staring at the feathered dart sticking out from between Lizzie's shoulder blades. She reached behind her, trying to grab it, but the dart was buried in exactly that part of her back that she couldn't reach. "Wha—" she said, turning toward them, and then her eyes rolled back, and she slumped on the ground.

Jake dove into the bushes as Filby hissed, "Come back, Hale! I had to do it!"

Jake hesitated, just long enough for Filby to push the leaves aside and shoot again. Jake dove aside, the dart narrowly missing him, and ran off through the bushes, scanning the ground furiously for tripwires or pits. Once he put a little distance between himself and Filby — the traitor! Filby! — he'd call Snakesman and the Colonel and bring the whole might of Stormglass down on —

Someone stepped out from behind a tree. A blond boy, maybe fifteen, holding a hockey stick casually against his shoulder. Jake swerved around, but his twin stepped out from behind another tree, also armed with a hockey stick. The twins both grinned at him madly.

The twin on the left swung his stick, and it struck Jake in the chest, knocking him clean off his feet. Jake slammed to the ground, and lay there gasping.

"Don't hurt him!" he heard Filby shouting. "Don't you dare hurt him, your grandfather will be furious!"

"Loser," the twin who'd hit him said, and spat on the ground next to his head.

Filby looked down at Jake's face, the tranquilizer pistol in his hand. "Sorry, new kid," he said. He even sounded like he meant it. But then again, he was pretty good at lying.

Filby pulled the trigger, and the dart struck Jake hard in the chest.

Jake woke up, his head fuzzy and dull. He moaned and tried to sit upright, but he couldn't. Something droned and hummed, and the hard floor beneath him rumbled and vibrated. Was he on an airplane? How long had he been unconscious? Where were they taking him? Where —

"He's waking up," a gruff voice said, and something pricked Jake in the arm — a needle — and he sank back into dim black clouds again.

The next time Jake woke up, he didn't move a muscle. He could tell his hands were bound behind him, but he wasn't sure about his legs. Maybe he could crack his eyes open just slightly, enough to see where he was being held —

"I know you're awake," Filby said, his voice nearby. "Your breathing changed. Don't feel bad. It's hard to fake being asleep. It takes practice."

Jake opened his eyes. "You faked being one of us," he said. "How much practice did that take?"

They were in a small room with cinderblock walls. Jake was tied up on his side on a concrete floor, and Filby sat on his heels a few feet away, watching him intently.

"Yes, I practiced," Filby said. "But I had to. Stormglass doesn't exactly treat its agents well. They sent you into dangerous situations with no training. Do you really think they care?"

"I guess they thought you and Lizzie would train me," Jake said, recovering. "Lizzie. Where is she?"

"Don't worry, she's fine. No one here will hurt her. Vindiqo believes in taking care of people."

"Then... where are we? There was an airplane..."

"We couldn't stay in Tanzania. Snakesman knew we were there, and we need to be left alone for a while."

Jake groaned. "All this time, you were the traitor. I thought it was Jenny."

Filby shook his head. "Jenny is as loyal as a dog. But you're not a dog, are you, Jake? You're new. Stormglass hasn't brainwashed you yet — I hope. You can still see reason. You don't have to be a prisoner here. Do you think being a secret agent is exciting? Imagine what it's like being a double agent."

"You want me to betray Stormglass? Like you did?" Jake would have spat at Filby's feet, if he hadn't been so thirsty.

Filby sighed. He sat down with his back against one of the familiar metal drums lining the wall.

"I haven't got a problem with loyalty, Hale. I've always been loyal. It's just that I was recruited by Vindiqo first."

THE TRAITOR'S TALE

"You've been working for Vindiqo all along?" Jake said, stunned. "Before Stormglass even recruited you?"

Filby nodded. "I've never told you my story, Hale, have I? When I was six years old, my mother and father were both killed in an accident. It happened unexpectedly. I was at school, and I guess I don't know why my parents were at home, instead of at the office, but a gas tank at home exploded and destroyed everything." Filby turned away, and looked as if he was wiping away a small tear. "They both worked at Vindiqo, and the company put the money together to send me to an orphanage. Have you ever lived in an orphanage, Hale?"

Jake shook his head.

"I don't know how others are, but this one was… unbearable. The teachers beat me, other kids beat me, it was the worst time in my life. And then, after what felt like years of this — maybe it was just a few months, I don't know — the company rescued me. A man and woman from Vindiqo came, saw what was happening, and they took me away."

Jake looked at Filby with pity, wondering if Vindiqo had sent him to that orphanage on purpose.

"They gave me a real family again. They took care of me." Filby's voice was dreamy and faraway. "And they taught me so much, Hale. How to hack computers, how to defend myself, how to fight, and escape, and tell lies, and shoot guns. They took me away from that terrible place, and gave me a new life."

"So how did you end up at Stormglass?"

"A couple of years ago, that man and that woman came to see me. They asked if I'd repay them for everything they'd done for me. They asked if I'd join Stormglass. I didn't want to — why would I want to go to Stormglass?"

"Because they're doing good? And trying to save the world?"

"That's what they claim, but it's not true. The Colonel is just angry with Vindiqo — it's some old rivalry or something. That's what they told me at Vindiqo. I didn't want to work for the Colonel, but I owed the company so much… I couldn't say no. So Vindiqo made some arrangements, and before long Stormglass rescued me from what they thought was an abusive foster family—"

"I think it was," Jake murmured, but Filby ignored him.

"Since then… I've been Agent Filby. And no one from Stormglass even suspected me." He almost sounded proud of himself. "My real name is Derren."

Jake closed his eyes. Filby had been… maybe not brainwashed, exactly, but he'd fallen for the lies. Jake needed his friend to see the truth.

"Filby, Derren, the stuff Vindiqo does... it's evil."

"They're not evil, Hale, that's just a Stormglass lie. Vindiqo is a business, and is making money, and, well, money can't buy you a family, but it comes close!"

"What about those sick twins? You think they aren't evil?"

Filby stopped, and frowned. "Yeah, they are weird. But they're related to someone important. They just need to learn some discipline and responsibility, that's all!"

Jake sighed. "Fine. Then what about the bees? Those things are vicious, Filby."

"But are they really?" Filby said. "What do we know for sure about the bees? They stung some cats to death, which was clearly a mistake. The bees were just being field-tested. That's why you test things, Hale, to see if they work! I'm sure the Doctor is working to make them safer."

"But they can be used to hold the world hostage — if countries don't buy the bees, they won't have food!"

"That's what you think," Filby said, almost gently. "But what proof do you have? All you know for sure is that the honeybees are dying. And that would mean the end of the world. So Vindiqo is fixing that problem by creating better bees. Remember what the beekeeper said, Hale — these bees are going to save the world! Vindiqo is going to save the world. And Stormglass is trying to stop them? That makes no sense. Even Lizzie said she thought Vindiqo's plan was brilliant."

"I think she said sick and deranged first," said Jake.

"Come on. You think developing super-bees doesn't cost a lot of money? Why shouldn't Vindiqo make their money back?"

"But they're programmed to kill normal bees," Jake said.

"Sometimes the weak have to die, to make room for the strong," Filby said, defensively.

Jake felt sick, and leaned back as Filby lightly kicked at one of the metal drums. Jake suddenly realized where he'd seen the drums before — on the Russian train, in the Argentinian base. Small letters were stenciled on the side, but he could only make out the word "attack." Attack pheromone? Why would Vindiqo need pheromones to kill their own bees?

Filby reached over and put his hand on Jake's shoulder. "Just give Vindiqo a chance, Hale. They might surprise you. You'll still get to work in the field, you'll still get to play with awesome gadgets, you'll still get to have fun, but you'll be paid, too. Join us, Hale. You'll be working for the winning team. At least talk to my boss—"

Jake relented. "Okay," he said.

PLAYING ALONG

Filby blinked. "What?"

Jake shrugged, as best he could with his hands tied. "Sure. Like you said, I just joined Stormglass a few days ago, and you're right — I don't really know anything about them, except what they've told me, and maybe I can't trust that. I'm not saying I'm going to join Vindiqo, because I don't know anything about them, either... but I like you, Filby, and you know a lot more about this than I do. And it's true I don't know what the Colonel is really up to. And that no one else has talked about paying me. If you say Vindiqo isn't so rotten, I'm at least willing to listen."

Filby grinned. "Hale, that's wonderful! I knew you'd see reason. Not like Lizzie. She tried to bite me when I gave her my pitch, can you believe that?"

Jake wriggled a little on the floor and tried not to grin at the thought of Lizzie trying to bite Filby. "Well, I promise not to bite. Is there any chance you could untie me?"

Filby looked at his face closely. "Just to warn you, if you try to knock me out and escape... it won't work."

"No tricks," Jake said — although, in fact, his entire plan had been to knock Filby over and run away, try to find Lizzie, and then escape. Maybe Jake should wait and figure out a better plan. "But my fingers are going numb, so I'd really like to be untied."

"Okay," Filby said. "I'm going to take you to meet the man who rescued me."

"The man who checked you out of the orphanage?"

Filby drew a wicked knife with a black, non-reflective blade and sliced through the plastic zip-ties holding Jake's hands and feet together. "That's right."

Jake stood up, rubbing his wrists, trying to massage feeling back into them.

"He's excited to meet you, Hale. He thinks you could do great things."

Filby led Jake from the storeroom down a narrow hallway with dirty white walls. Jake put his hands into his pockets, casually — and felt his trick coins. Filby must have forgotten about those, which meant Jake wasn't entirely defenseless. Not that he could see how a listening device or the noises of a violent battle would help him now, but maybe, maybe…. They passed two other closed doors, and Jake thought he heard muffled sounds behind one of them — could Lizzie be trapped in there?

Filby stopped before a door at the end of the hall and knocked on it three times sharply.

A smooth, cultured voice said, "Come in."

Filby opened the door and gestured for Jake to enter. The room was messy, an office with a desk holding a widescreen computer monitor and jumbled papers. A long window behind the desk looked out on a vast warehouse filled with beehives, a seemingly endless expanse, far larger than the operation in Argentina.

A man in an immaculate lab coat stood before the window, his back to Jake, hands clasped behind him. When Filby shut the door, the man turned to face the boys.

It was Doctor Horst.

THE DOCTOR

The Doctor laughed, reaching one hand out across the desk to Jake. "It's good to see you again, young agent Hale."

They shook hands, and Jake noticed he only had nine fingers — the man's left pinky was missing. Jake sank into the plastic-and-metal chair across from the desk, and the Doctor took a seat on the other side. A low murmur of voices emerged from a pair of speakers next to the computer, and he leaned forward and turned down the volume. "Forgive the mess," the Doctor said, pushing aside a heap of papers, making a few of them fall to the floor. "I have a brilliant mind, but I'm a bit disorganized sometimes. I'm also missing some of my socks. You don't happen to have my bag still, do you?"

Jake shook his head nervously.

"A pity. And my Tolstoy novel, *War and Peace*?"

Jake again shook his head.

"So sad. Can you believe, I never actually found out how it ends."

He picked up a paper, distractedly glanced over it, and then let it drop to the table.

"So how will it end?" the Doctor asked, raising one massive eyebrow. "I do hate war, with its bloodshed and misery. It's ugly. Peace is so much better, don't you think? It's filled with kindness, happiness, untold riches… yes, I do care about money. I'm sorry if that makes me evil. Does it?"

Jake shook his head, no.

"Well, you, young Hale, you could join me in the untold riches." He quieted his voice to a whisper, "Derren, who you know as Filby, will soon be a millionaire. And he's only fourteen. You could become one, too. What would you do with a million dollars, Hale?"

Jake leaned back into the chair, and spent a few awkward seconds picturing himself as a millionaire — but the memory of the Beekeeper brought him back to reality.

"What about Lizzie," Jake asked. "What will happen to her?"

"Mmm," the Doctor said, looking at Jake thoughtfully. "Good question. We'll keep trying to make her see some sense, of course. She's a smart kid, but she's headstrong. To be perfectly honest — and I will always be honest with you, Hale — I don't think she's willing to listen. She's been too brainwashed by the Colonel to see the truth."

"So what will happen to her, then?"

"Oh, it would be revealed that she led you into this terrible trap, that she ruined the mission, and so on and so forth. We'll deposit large sums of money into her father's bank account, so it'll be obvious she was working for us. She won't be harmed at all, and she'll make quite a bit of money out of it, but her days as a Stormglass agent will be over."

"I guess that's fair," Jake said. "So what would I have to do?"

"Why, that's the best part about this whole operation, Hale. You wouldn't have to anything! You'd return to Stormglass along with Agent Filby here. You'll have found nothing suspicious in the African base, and — once we've successfully released our bee program — you'll profit in untold ways." He shifted some papers around purposefully, and held up the one he was looking for. "Here, we're ready to open a bank account in your name, a secret bank account of course, and start letting the riches flow in." He paused, smiling paternally, before continuing. "One day, we might ask a little favor. Nothing bad, of course, but maybe for some information, or a teensy bit of—"

The door burst open, and the assistant rushed in, breathing hard. "Doctor, I need to speak to you—"

"I'm in a meeting, young man!" Jake's stomach shriveled at his suddenly threatening voice.

"But sir, Mr. Kim is here! He wants to speak—"

"Shhh," the Doctor snapped, rising, then smiled at the boys. "Hale, I'm so terribly sorry about this rude interruption. You seem to have arrived at such a busy time — an important client to meet with, an important operation to oversee, the bees to keep happy — it really is the perfect storm, you see. Derren, do keep Hale company. Tell him about your life here, how nice it's been since that terrible time at the unfortunate orphanage. And don't worry, boys, I'll be back soon to continue our discussion. We'll talk about just how rich Hale could become." The Doctor squeezed Jake's shoulder as he passed. Instinctively, at that same moment, Jake slipped one of his listening-device coins into the Doctor's jacket pocket. It was so stealthy, that no one noticed a thing.

The assistant bustled out of the room with the Doctor at his heels, and as soon as the door shut Jake rushed to the other side of the desk and started rifling through papers.

"What are you doing?" Filby asked, alarmed.

"What I'm trained to do. Looking for intel on your, maybe our, boss!" Jake turned over pieces of paper, but they were mostly charts about honey production or densely scientific stuff, nothing marked anything useful like "Deadly Global Takeover Plan."

The monitor on the desk caught Jake's eye. The screen was divided into four quadrants, all showing video footage, presumably from security cameras in different parts of the facility: a laboratory where technicians were doing something with beakers of chemicals, some kind of library — he froze. Was it Stormglass? Was that Cyrus Rex?

"Did you see—?" he asked Filby, but it was too late, and he needed to find what he was looking for. Another quadrant showed a room full of empty bunk beds, and then a conference room with an Asian man sitting behind a long table. The Doctor and his assistant came into view in that room, and the Doctor reached out a hand.

"Filby, do you have a Stormpad?" Jake said.

He frowned. "Yes, but it won't work. This facility has jammers. You're not getting out, Hale."

"That's fine. I want to listen to something from inside. I planted a listening device on the Doctor."

Filby gaped. "You bugged him? The Doctor? Are you crazy? You're going to get us—"

TRUE INTENTIONS

Jake looked at Filby levelly. "You disapprove? What, is spying on your boss against the rules?"

The traitor blushed, then frowned. "It's just — he's the man who—"

"If you're so sure he doesn't have evil plans, what's the harm?" Jake said. "If he's talking to his assistant about making the world a better place, then I'll admit I was wrong, and I'll go along with whatever you want. Besides, do you think the Doctor would hesitate to spy on you if he wanted?"

Filby sighed. "If it will help you see reason, Hale, fine. I'm sure Doctor Horst has nothing to hide." He drew the Stormpad from one of his pockets and handed it to Jake so he could log in. Jake activated it with his handprint, then swiped the little icon of a coin with an ear drawn on it as Filby said, "I'm sure they're just discussing—"

"So wonderful to meet you in person, Mr. Kim," the Doctor's voice said from the Stormpad. "I have to say, I'm a great fan of your work."

"Your assistant was showing me the hives, and they're very good. I am ready to invest in your bees."

"Wonderful." The Doctor sat down. "When will you need them?"

"In one month," Kim said, calmly folding his arms across his chest. "This event will remind the world: you don't mess with Kim Kyok-un."

Filby gasped at the screen, and spat out, "That's Kim Kyok-un?"

The name sounded familiar, but Jake couldn't remember from where.

"You don't know him? He's been in hiding for years, and he's on every most-wanted list in the world. Remember, Stormglass uncovered his plot — oh, you weren't with Stormglass. He'd tried to set off explosives at the Olympics. But why would the Doctor be doing business with him? He's a terrorist!"

They both turned back to the screen.

"I presume you'd like them carrying sarin?"

"Of course, that's what I'd like. But sarin is so poisonous. It will not kill your bees?"

"Oh, these bees can carry anything — they're almost perfect. Of course, you're paying for that perfection, but you'll quickly discover it's worth it. The bee bellies — the venom sacs — are practically made of steel. And speaking of steel, I'll also provide several steel drums of attack pheromone."

"I'm sorry, I don't understand. Can you speak to me so I can understand?"

"Haha. Sorry — we've produced a liquid that tells the bees where to attack." *That's what's in the metal barrels*, thought Jake. "The bees smell the phe-, the, er, attack juice from far away, very far away. What is your planned target?"

"A place where you play the American football."

"A stadium? A large one?"

"One of the largest."

"Fantastic. I think two dozen tanks of the pheromone should be more than enough. You'll just have to spray the seats before the game, and the scent will rub off on the clothes of the spectators. The bees will attack, mercilessly. You know that everyone in the stadium will die, right?"

"Of course. After Stormglass found out about my Olympics plan—"

"Yes, I know the very group you mean," cursed the Doctor. "I too have a vendetta. But let's not worry about them. I have plans for a small act of revenge," he said. Mr. Kim laughed, and Dr. Horst laughed, and they both laughed loudly as if this was an old joke between them — even though they'd only just met. As they stood and shook hands, the Doctor wiped his eyes and asked one final question. "What stadium will you be targeting, by the way?"

"A stadium in San Francisco," he said. Jake gulped as Mr. Kim said, "The team that is named for a number."

"Do you mean the 49ers?" asked the Doctor.

"Yes, yes," laughed Mr. Kim.

"I guess you'll be kicking off this football season with a bit of a bang."

Jake's stomach knotted up as the two of them laughed louder, shook hands and Mr. Kim left the room. That was his team, his father's team. The stadium could fit 70,000 people, people he'd know, friends of his, maybe even him and his dad!

Jake turned to Filby and grabbed his arm, "Okay, smart guy, explain how that's going to save the world!"

"Quiet," hushed Filby, pointing to the screen. The Doctor and his assistant were now alone.

"Kim is sold," the Doctor said to himself, his voice filled with glee, then turned to his assistant. "I'm rich, you're rich, we're both rich beyond belief!"

"But what about Stormglass?" asked the assistant.

"Ha! The planes are loaded, and ready to set off. In just hours, Mundt will set off the electromagnetic pulse and destroy all the Stormglass computers and defense systems. Everything at Stormglass will shut down!"

"How did Mundt smuggle an EMP into Stormglass? That would be impossible!"

"Not if it was implanted in his prosthetic arm, it isn't," laughed the Doctor. "The machinery in that arm is so complex, it would take an expert to recognize the EMP. And Stormglass prisons are in the most secure part of their headquarters, right next to their computer mainframe! After Mundt sets the EMP off, that's when we'll send in the bees."

"But surely Stormglass has backup power systems in place," the assistant said. "They—"

"Don't presume to tell me how to run an operation," the Doctor snapped. "This is why I needed Derren. Their sweet agent Filby uploaded a virus that has silently disabled all of the backup systems."

The assistant shook his head as the Doctor chuckled. "It's hard to believe a boy so young would willingly send all those people to their deaths—"

"Oh, he has no idea."

Jake glanced at Filby, but his expression was impossible to read. He was listening intently, though — Jake could see that.

"Without their security, we'll be able to break in through one of the hidden runways, fill their headquarters with aerosolized attack pheromone, and release the bees. Yes, so that will kill them all. Ahem, little Derren also uploaded fake reports in the Stormglass computers, showing that they were experimenting with a new form of bee. The StormBee, as it will surely be known in headlines across the world, will be discovered to have been destroying the world's honey supply."

"Who would believe this, though?" asked the pale assistant.

"Everyone will," the Doctor laughed. "Vindiqo owns enough of the media to make this story the truth!"

"But why Stormglass?"

"They've been trying to bring down my program from day one. It was Cyrus Rex and his little investigators that took away my medical degrees, who stole my right to practice medicine! They couldn't see what I was doing. They cared only about petty morality, seeing the world in black and white — while I was actually saving the world! When this massacre is investigated, Stormglass will be blamed for destroying themselves in a biological accident. Cyrus Rex will be blamed for the death of thousands! And, after Mr. Kim releases the bees at the football stadium, that number will be even higher!"

"But there's a problem," the assistant said. "What about Mundt?"

"What about him?"

"He's inside Stormglass headquarters now. How will he avoid being killed by the bees?"

"Why, for the past two months he's been taking that special supplement you created, the anti-bee pill."

There was a long pause. "Doctor... you know I never made such a thing, and that such a thing is impossible."

"Of course I know that," the Doctor laughed, "but Mundt doesn't. He believes in the power of science — and he believes in me. He'll be surprised when the bees begin to sting him, I'm sure — but not for long. It's a shame to waste such a useful tool, but I would sacrifice a hundred men like Mundt to strike such a decisive blow against the agency that crippled me."

"You do so much to inspire loyalty in your employees, Doctor," the assistant said nervously.

The Doctor wasn't listening, but instead was raising his arms as if addressing a crowd of spectators. "The public bees will be the salvation of the human race," he announced. "And the private bees will be the damnation! And I'll be the one in control! And we will all be rich beyond belief."

"Well, I can live with that," the assistant said with a smile. "What will you do with the children?"

"I'll either pay them off, or I'll kill them," the Doctor said. "All three of them. I haven't really decided yet." He started laughing. "Oh, who am I kidding? I've already decided."

"So this is why you had the boy's parents killed? You've been planning this for seven years?"

"Yes, I needed my mole."

"Enough!" Filby shouted, and actually pressed the palms of his hands over his ears. Jake turned the volume on his Stormpad down. The Doctor was deranged. And all of this — the dead bee, the clues, Mundt, Filby's parents — had been a trap?

Filby turned his back and trembled all over — was he crying? Shaking with rage? Jake started to reach out to touch his shoulder, then drew back, afraid that if he touched Filby, the double agent might explode... or collapse.

"They lied to you, Filby," he said instead, as gently as he could. "They used you. I know you wouldn't have gone along with it if you'd known they wanted to... to do all this. They—"

"I know that," Filby said. "I understand the implications. I'm very smart, Hale. Yes, they tricked me. The question now is: what am I going to do to punish them for it?"

SMOKE AND FIRE

Filby turned around, and though there were tears in his eyes, he didn't look sad — he looked angry. He stalked across the room, and kicked at a closet door until he splintered the wood, then wrenched it open. "Your gear's in here, and so is Lizzie's. The stun gun, too." He turned and tossed a key to Jake. "She's locked in a storage room down the hallway. Get her free, find a way to contact Stormglass HQ." He made a face. "You know what to do, Hale."

"What are you going to do?"

"I'm going to fix the damage I caused," he said. "Don't worry about the bees here. I'll take care of them. You save Stormglass."

Before Jake could stop him, Filby wrenched open the door and raced out.

Jake hauled his gear out of the closet and turned on his own Stormpad. He tried to contact Snakesman, and then tried his direct line to Cyrus Rex, but neither worked — the Stormpad screen just said, "Connection failed."

He was on his own again. Jake hurried down the hallway, hoping all the guards were busy preparing for the assault on Stormglass.

He unlocked the door in the hallway, then jumped out of the way as Lizzie tried to kick him in the groin.

She was on the ground on her back, a gag in her mouth, hands bound behind her, and ankles zip-tied too, but that hadn't stopped her from positioning herself so she could attack the first person through the door. Her eyes widened when she saw Jake, and he undid her gag and used the knife from his bag to cut her restraints.

"Filby!" she hissed. "That slimy little traitor!"

"I know," Jake said. "But he's with us again — he gave me our gear and let me go."

Lizzie frowned. "What, he's a triple agent?"

"Something like that," Jake said. "I'll explain later. We need to move." He told her, as fast as he could, what he'd heard of the Doctor's plan: the bees and the pheromones — and the electromagnetic pulse hidden in Mundt's prosthetic arm.

Lizzie switched into smoothly professional mode. "Okay. If Filby's handling the bees here, we have to handle the bees elsewhere. Let's hope we can reach them before they leave. First, we could use some intel about what kind of facility we're in."

"I noticed a little map of the building in Horst's office, with the emergency exits marked," Jake said. "Would that help?"

"Glad they're concerned about fires," Lizzie snarled. "That might be helpful for everyone. Let's go."

"This is where we are," Lizzie said, touching her finger to the laminated Vindiqo map on the wall in Horst's office, while Jake stood at the mostly-closed door, peering through the crack to watch the hall. "There's an exit down there. Aha, marked in English and French. So we're probably in Canada. Think, Michelle, think."

Jake glanced back at her with a raised eyebrow. "Michelle?" She glared back for a split second, before focusing on the map again.

"Think, Lizzie, think! Assuming we're in French-speaking Canada, we must be in Quebec. So how would they get the bees to America? Cars, too small. A truck. Really? A truckload of deadly bees? Way too tricky with tight border control. Trains are just stupid. So they're flying."

"Could they have their own airstrip," said Jake, remembering the number of private airstrips he'd seen in the last few days.

"Yes! They must. Okay, Hale, let's go."

"Okay," Jake said, turning toward her — and then stopped, staring out the long window that overlooked the hives. "Lizzie, look."

She turned, and whistled.

The beehives, almost all the endless rows of them, were on fire. Jake glimpsed a figure in a white beekeeper suit hurling an improvised bomb at a distant hive, and when the bottle of gasoline struck, fire bloomed. The scene was eerie, more so for being totally silent — the glass must have been soundproof. There were a few bees buzzing listlessly about near the glass, but the smoke was making them drop to the ground, and as Jake watched, more fireballs burst.

"That's got to be Filby," Jake said.

"I'm impressed," Lizzie said. "I didn't think he had it in him. He's doing his part, so let's do ours, and fast. That kind of destruction won't go unnoticed for long."

Jake hesitated, watching the window glass turn black as the room beyond filled with smoke. "But how will he get away..."

"He's an agent, Hale. He'll find a way."

They hurried down the hall, through a heavy metal door, and dashed down another corridor. They turned a corner, where a startled woman in a lab coat stared at them, wide-eyed. Lizzie didn't even slow down, just waved and said, "Aren't *Take Your Kid to Work* days cool?"

The next door took them outside, into blazing afternoon light. They were in a heavily forested area, beautiful really, and Jake flashed back to a camping trip with his parents. When had he last called them? Would they be worried yet? Would he ever even see them again?

Lizzie scanned the area, then grabbed his arm. "There's an aircraft hangar, and a runway beyond." They crouched and ran for the tree line, then behind the trees, looping around toward the long metal hangar. Someone shouted, and they ducked down, Lizzie peering through her binoculars.

"They're running toward the lab," she said. "It's totally on fire. Let's get into the hangar while we can."

They crept up to the side of the building, where Lizzie eased open a door and stuck her head inside for a second.

"Damn!" she hissed, back to the wall. "There are two planes, fast ones. One's taxiing. The other is still being loaded. This is bad." She opened her bag and slipped out a small object: four black rubber rings welded together, each tipped with a small metal spike. She slipped them over the fingers of her left hand, then withdrew an identical set, and put them on her right.

"What are those?"

"They're brass knuckles," she said. "Except they're not brass — they're stun knuckles."

"Are you supposed to have those?"

"Not really, no."

She flexed her hands, and blue arcs of electricity sparked on top of the rings, sizzling between the metal spikes. She slipped back into the hangar, rushing toward the aircraft, a low-slung, needle-nosed plane with backwards-sweeping wings. Lizzie hid underneath the fuselage by the landing gear, and when a man came down the steps from inside the plane, she kept crouching, waiting for him to leave. Once he was on the far side of the hangar, his back to them, she beckoned to Jake, who raced across to join her, and they sneaked into the plane together.

Inside was just cargo space filled with crates, and white canisters fitted with spray nozzles, and numerous stacked wooden boxes. As they crept past the wooden boxes, Jake realized they were buzzing.

"Hives," he mouthed to Lizzie. She nodded. They were tied up with rope and wrapped in layers of plastic, but filled with buzzing bees. Long rectangular pieces of mesh covered the openings, and Jake could see the bugs writhing around, trying to find a way out. This was too close to the insects. Jake shivered.

Two pilots climbed on board, and took seats up front, running through their preflight checklists. Lizzie took the tranquilizer gun out of her bag and counted the darts. There were two. She started to creep forward. Jake wasn't sure what she had planned, but it wasn't going to be good for the pilots.

Suddenly voices shouted from outside. "Let's go! We're wheels up in five minutes! We've got a tight schedule!"

"Damn," Lizzie mouthed. She nodded her head to the back, and led the way in between the hives, disappearing among the rows of stacked crates and metal tanks. Jake followed, wriggling through cracks too small for an adult to fit through. They found a space between the wall and a crate and crouched there. Jake was relieved to be away from the bees, until he read the bold stenciled type on the side of the crate. *Explosives: Handle With Care.* On the sides of the drums he could now read the full text: *V25-17: Attack Pheromone.* He was exhausted. As the engines revved up, the hold was filled with noise.

"What's the plan?" Jake whispered, finally able to communicate.

"I wish I had one," Lizzie whispered back. "At least we're on the plane. We can try to reach

Stormglass again once we're in the air, away from the signal jamming."

"So we just... stow away?"

"I'm open to better suggestions," she said, and then went silent, because a lot of people were climbing onto the plane, their boots thudding, one of them barking orders about securing weapons and finding seats.

Then one voice announced, "Doctor Horst, are you sure you want to come with us? We're not expecting much resistance, but I can't promise you there won't be a fight."

"You think I'd miss this?" Horst said peevishly. "This is seven years of vengeance. I wouldn't miss this for the world."

There was a clunk as the airplane door was secured, and a moment later, the plane began to move.

FLIGHT OF THE VIPERBEES

Jake and Lizzie didn't dare speak. Horst sounded close.

As the plane taxied out of the hangar and began to zoom down the runway, Lizzie took out her Stormpad and opened a text chat channel to Jake's pad.

'You think Filby's okay?,' she wrote.

Jake shook his head, then tapped. 'I don't know. Fire looked bad. But he's experienced, right?'

'I wish he was here,' she wrote. 'Even if he's a quadruple agent or something he was always better at waiting than I am.'

'So let's not wait. Let's do something.' He paused, then typed again. 'What can we do?'

'We could hijack the plane,' she wrote.

'Can you fly one of these?'

'Sure I can, I've done it loads of times.'

'Really?'

Lizzie shrugged. 'Only simulators, but I'd bet it's the same.'

Jake shook his head emphatically. 'I do not like that idea.'

'Come on, there are worse things than plane crashes.'

'Like what?'

They lifted off, leaning against the crates and bracing themselves as the jet accelerated upward. 'Fasten seatbelt,' Lizzie typed, then gave him a wink. But of course, they didn't have seatbelts. Or even seats. Jake didn't want to think about plane crashes right then.

'If this plane crashes,' he typed, 'the hives would break open, and the attack juice too. So we'd be trapped in a wreck with murder-bees. That's way worse than an ordinary plane crash.'

Lizzie rolled her eyes. 'Flying is easy, though. Takeoffs are kind of tricky, but they're doing that for us.'

'And landings?'

'Um… landings are the hardest.'

Jake shook his head again. 'Too dangerous, Lizzie, and too many soldiers. We'd lose the whole element of surprise.'

Lizzie tapped at her screen forcefully. 'Element of surprise only good if we do something surprising!'

Jake nodded. 'I have one idea. Can you work these sprayers?' He pointed to one of the canisters.

Lizzie nodded.

Jake gave her a thumbs up. But before he could type out his plan, Doctor Horst shouted to the pilot, "Who's on the radio? Is there any word about those damn kids?"

"That was the Chairman, sir. All three Stormglass agents are still on the loose. The men are searching, along with the Chairman's grandchildren. God help those agents if the twins find them."

"God help those three kids if I find them," Horst said.

Jake was relieved to hear Filby had escaped, and wondered if he would try to warn Stormglass. Did Filby even have his Stormpad? He was probably just trying to escape. It was up to Jake and Lizzie to save their headquarters.

"Sir, you should stay seated. For your safety!"

"I'm making sure my hives are secure," Horst said.

"Sir, my men know how to tie down cargo."

"Oh, yes, I'm sure. And if one of these hives falls over and releases the bees? It would be a stingfest. In the most unfortunate way."

Lizzie and Jake froze as Horst moved among the hives, crouching and muttering to himself. Jake thought the bees started buzzing more loudly as the bee scientist fussed over them, but that had to be his imagination, right? The scientist took his time, too. Jake desperately wanted to try and contact Cyrus Rex on his Stormpad, but he was afraid to so much as move — let alone speak — with the enemy so close. If they were discovered now, all was lost. Jake could see Horst's dirty lab coat in a crack between the crates... and Horst stayed there, in the center of the stacked hives, cooing to his bees, whispering to them as if they were his best friends and not colonies of insects bred for murder. Maybe they were his best friends. Or his only ones.

After an unbearably long time, the voice shouted over the noise of the plane, "Doctor, we're landing soon! If you'd strap in, that would be better."

Horst swore at him, but rose and lumbered away. It sounded like he was further away, at the front of the plane.

Jake exhaled for what felt like the first time in hours.

"Contact Stormglass!" Lizzie hissed. "Quick!"

Jake turned on his Stormpad and called Cyrus Rex on his direct line. This time, the call went through, and Rex's face appeared on the screen, grave and concerned. "Agent Hale? Where are you? Report your status."

"My status is pretty lousy, sir," Jake said, whispering hoarsely, though he thought the noise of the engines would probably make his voice inaudible where the enemy agents were seated. "Doctor Horst is on his way to attack Stormglass, with soldiers and bees, and he's landing right now—"

"What did you say?" Rex said, alarmed.

"Filby was—"

Suddenly the screen went black, Colonel Rex's face disappearing. Jake tried to call again, and then tried to reach Snakesman, but had no luck. The connection to headquarters had been severed.

"Lizzie," Jake whispered, looking up from his blank screen. "I can't get through at all. I think Mundt set off his electromagnetic pulse."

Lizzie grimaced. "That's bad. Did he understand you?"

"I'm not sure," Jake admitted.

"Let's hope he heard you," Lizzie said nervously. "But just in case, tell me about this plan!"

PHEROMONE ATTACK

The small plane landed surprisingly smoothly in the desert. Lizzie and Jake crouched nervously amid the explosive crates, with her holding a canister of the bee attack pheromone, waiting for the right moment.

"Move, move, move!" the commander shouted. "Secure the perimeter and watch for Stormglass sentries. Their base should be in chaos right now, so take advantage of the confusion! No, Barnett, put that stupid outfit down — we don't need the bee suits until we're ready to release the bugs. It'll only slow you down! Doctor Horst, sir, you should stay here until it's safe."

"Don't tell me what to do," the Doctor whispered to himself. "This is my operation."

Jake gave Lizzie a small grin. They listened as the soldiers and Horst tromped down the stairs. Lizzie stood up, carrying the canister, and Jake followed her through the crates. He had the tranquilizer gun in one hand, in case the pilots came running back from the cockpit, and smoke bombs at his belt, in case their plan went badly wrong.

Lizzie rushed to the top of the stairs leading off the plane. She held the canister at her waist, and let out a yell.

"Ready for a bath?" she screamed. She held down the trigger on the nozzle, and sprayed a jet of attack pheromone over the eight soldiers as they tried to cover their faces. Doctor Horst was nowhere to be seen. One of the soldiers reached for his pistol, but Lizzie stood firm. "I don't think so!" She pointed to the beehive directly behind her. "You really want to shoot that into a plane full of beehives, when you're covered in this stuff?" She wiggled the canister, and sprayed more. The man hesitated, his eyes wide in sudden terror.

Jake lifted one of the bee-filled hives. "Put your guns on the ground, now, or I throw the box!"

The commander barked at his men to drop their weapons, and a rain of metal fell, pistols and a couple of assault rifles clattering to the ground. Jake scanned the horizon. Where was Horst?

"Now step away from the guns, there you go, just keep backing up. I'm going to count to thirty, and then he's throwing this hive out of the plane, guys. You'd really better start running!"

The Commander glared at Lizzie, as if he wanted to kill her, then he turned and set off running at a terrific clip, his men fanning out behind him.

"We're not really throwing it, right?" Jake whispered to Lizzie, tightening his grip on the hive. "If these bees get out in the wild—"

"Right," Lizzie said. "I'm not allowed to crash planes. I'm not allowed to start an ecological apocalypse. I never get to have any fun." Jake set the hive down carefully, as Lizzie turned to the cockpit.

"Okay, pilots, you can stop hiding and come on out. We've got weapons, so don't try anything cute."

The pilot and co-pilot rushed out, crouched low — understandable, with the hives of bees stacked behind their enemies. They didn't even pause, just ran after the others.

Lizzie sighed. "We'd better get out of here before they realize we didn't toss out any bees."

"Bomb the bees?" Jake suggested.

"Totally. Set the timer for, like, now. It's going to get smoky in here."

Jake set the timer on a canister of poisonous smoke, placed it among the hives, then followed Lizzie down the stairs into the hot desert air. The clutter of guns still sat outside the plane.

"Shall we take the guns," suggested Jake.

"No, we never use guns," said Lizzie. "But we need to make sure they don't come back for them. How..."

In a moment of inspiration, Jake grabbed one of the hives, and carefully placed it on top of the pile. "They're covered in attack juice. Let's see them come back now," he said.

Lizzie smiled wide. "You're really turning into something, new kid. Now run!"

Off in the distance, they could see the other plane. Lizzie crouched low and bolted toward the shelter of a pile of boulders. Jake followed her, wondering if the fleeing Vindiqo soldiers would head to the second plane, or if the fear of the bees would keep them running through the desert for a while.

"Do you have a plan?" Jake asked breathlessly as they ducked behind the rocks.

"Plan?" Lizzie said. "No. I thought you did!"

He shook his head. "That was as far as it went."

"What about those explosives back on the plane?"

"Wait – you can play with dynamite but not guns? Let's stay away from the boom-booms," Jake said. "How about that no-driver car, what's her name, Hermes?"

Lizzie's eyes went wide. "That's right! She's kept in a garage aboveground — away from the EMP! Her systems won't be fried." Lizzie yanked out her Stormpad and started hitting buttons. "We can steer her like a remote-controlled car."

"Let's see if we can create a distraction, then," Jake said.

"YOU ARE SURROUNDED," boomed the amplified speakers hidden in Hermes's front grille.

There were three men carrying canisters of attack pheromone gas and bulky beehives from the other plane, across the sand, and they froze. Hermes roared toward them, remotely piloted by Lizzie with her Stormpad. She and Jake were concealed in a growth of scraggly brush. Jake hurled the coin that made horrific battle noises in one direction, and tossed a flash-bang coin in the other. The resulting cacophony — like a gunfight and demolition derby happening inside your head, it was so loud — came from all directions and the three men scattered madly on random courses, abandoning the hives and canisters, certain they were about to be killed by something but not sure what.

Lizzie screamed.

"Come on, Lizzie, they're not that loud," Jake yelled, pulling out a second flash-bang coin. But Lizzie didn't reply. He swerved around and discovered why.

Doctor Horst held one arm around Lizzie's throat, and a gun to her head. His hair was a mess, and he was covered in dirt, and he wheezed as if he'd been running. But under those massive eyebrows, his eyes remained the ice cool blue calm they always were.

"Yes, it's a gun," Horst spat out "You absurd little children. I could have given you a new life — one free from guilt and fear. I could have given you money! Respect! Honor!" Jake watched a bubble forming at the side of the Doctor's mouth as he ranted, and remembered Lizzie's warning of a million year ago — only fight someone with a gun if you're pretty sure you're going to die – and he realized, this is when he was pretty sure he was going to die. Lizzie's eyes flicked nervously downward as if she was trying to tell Jake something.

His pockets were empty. He didn't have the guns. He watched the crazy Doctor and felt an empty pit in his stomach, and wished there had been more time for training. Lizzie's eyes kept flicking down, as the Doctor sneered.

"You could have chosen life with Vindiqo, and yet you're choosing death with Stormglass. I'm so confused as to why? What would lead you to this?"

Jake looked into Lizzie's eyes, and suddenly realized where she was looking: at his hand. He was still holding a coin... the last flash-bang coin! And this was his time to do something crazy.

"Tell me, Doctor," Jake interrupted. "Do you like magic?"

The Doctor had barely lifted his massive eyebrows in confusion before Jake twisted the coin, and the world exploded in blinding light and deafening noise. The Doctor flinched away with a gasp, giving Lizzie enough space to twist — she whipped her arm around her body, and in one split second slammed a knuckleduster-fist into the Doctor's face. Sparks exploded as contact was made, and Horst screamed in pain, stumbled backward, and collapsed twitching and trembling to the ground.

Lizzie stood over his body, and held her fist like a boxer about to start round two. "Do you need another, you deranged quack?" she cried in anger, as more sparks popped from her hand.

Horst's bubbling mouth twisted into a grimace. "You're too late," he mumbled as a wet patch spread through his trousers. "This is all so completely... pointless."

There was a huge explosion — and that wasn't part of their distraction plan. The blast came from the entrance to Hangar X, which was hidden in a heap of boulders. One of the men must have blown the hangar door open.

Jake helped tie up Horst's arms and feet, then Lizzie steered Hermes back to them. The doors popped open, and they scrambled inside. Hermes roared off toward the source of the explosion.

"I sure wish we had the tranquilizer gun right now," Lizzie said, steering jerkily while Jake wiped away the dusty windshield. The hangar door had been blown outward, the metal shredded and the boulders surrounding it blown apart. Four more Vindiqo soldiers, armed with assault rifles, crouched some distance away, waiting for the smoke to clear.

They looked up when Hermes began to approach, and one of them aimed an assault rifle and opened fire. Lizzie screamed, and the Stormpad flew to the floor. Jake grabbed it, and furiously slid his fingers along the screen to make the car take evasive maneuvers. The car flung both of them back and forth in their seats.

"We're not bulletproof!" Lizzie shouted.

"We really should be!" he shouted back. "Put that in the suggestion box!"

Jake caught a glimpse of movement from the direction of the hangar door, and the gunfire stopped. One of the Vindiqo men started screaming, and they all scattered, running wildly away into the desert.

A pair of fast-moving, dark shapes leapt out from beyond the remains of the hangar door, streaking off after the fleeing attackers. They looked like dogs, but were fast as cheetahs, their motion eerie and unnatural. Two dozen Stormglass agents in dark gray body armor streamed out of the hangar after them, fanning out to surround the enemy. Jake shouted a cry of victory and Lizzie screeched the vehicle to a stop.

She turned to him with an honest smile. "I guess the Colonel got your message after all," she said, laughing.

DEBRIEF

A man emerged from the hangar, dressed in a helmet and a bulletproof vest. He strolled over to Hermes and knocked on the passenger window with his knuckles.

Lizzie and Jake climbed out. "Welcome home, agents," he said, lifting his visor. It was Snakesman, armed and ready for combat. "Hungary was a red herring, just an empty building. How about Africa? And where's Filby?"

"He's... making his own way home," Jake said.

Snakesman grunted. "I'll need a fuller explanation of that statement soon. For now I'll take an immediate situation report, please."

"We've got a mad bee scientist tied up nearby," Lizzie said. "By one plane are a pile of guns, one live bee hive, and a bunch of other bees who are, we hope, already dead."

"Bees?" Snakesman said, and whistled. "Vindiqo brought a present for us? So kind..."

"I know, it was supposed to be a killer of a surprise," said Lizzie.

Snakesman shook his head. "That's nasty, even for them."

"There's also a terrified squad of unarmed soldiers running through the desert in that direction, so, you know — keep an eye out." Lizzie shaded her eyes and surveyed the scene of smoke and destruction. "Otherwise, you seem to have things under control. Nice hustle here, sir." Armed Stormglass agents ran through the badlands.

"When a trusted agent says headquarters is about to be invaded, we take it seriously," Snakesman said dryly. "Especially when the entire computer system goes down moments later."

"Mundt had an electromagnetic pulse weapon," Jake said, "hidden in his mechanical arm!"

Snakesman squeezed his eyes closed and grunted, slapping his own face.

"Our facility is hardened against electromagnetic pulses that come from outside, not inside. Someone will have to do something about that."

"Can I go help chase down bad guys?" Lizzie said.

Snakesman shook his head. "You've done enough chasing for now. And don't think I don't see those things on your knuckles, Lizzie. Those are not authorized Stormgadgets. Right now, I think the two of you should come have a talk with the Colonel."

Lizzie gaped. "What? For wearing non-regulation knuckledusters, I have to get hauled in front of the Colonel—"

Snakesman rolled his eyes. "No, Agent Lew, you're not being reprimanded. I'm fairly sure the Colonel wants to promote you. Both of you."

"This is not a formal debriefing." Colonel Rex gazed at them over the rim of a teacup in one of the darkened conference rooms, now lit only by emergency lighting. He took a slow sip. "We'll have time for that later. But I want to be filled in on a few things right away. You completed the special assignment I gave you, Hale?"

"Filby was the traitor," Jake said, and saw Lizzie flinch out of the corner of his eye. "Though I didn't really discover him. I didn't even seriously suspect him, until he betrayed us." Jake told the Colonel and Lizzie about Kim and the plot against the football game, and Filby's story, about how he was an orphan raised by Vindiqo, and how Filby had tried to redeem himself.

"He fooled all of us," Rex said. "But not as badly as he was fooled himself."

Jake shrugged. "I hope he comes back. He'll need protection from Vindiqo after he destroyed their lab."

"He's earned a certain amount of forgiveness by doing that," Colonel Rex said. "With Doctor Horst in custody, along with the only surviving specimens of his insects, it's unlikely Vindiqo will be able to market their bees any time soon. That particular danger is behind us for now. And because of your investigations, Hale, we now know Kim Kyok-un is in Canada — and we're prepared for any terrorist attacks on the 49ers."

"I can't believe he was lying to me all along," Lizzie said, shaking her head. "The whole time we were together. Sometimes he was kind of annoying, but to be a traitor..."

Colonel Rex shook his head. "In Filby's mind, he was being loyal to the people who took care of him. The ones who gave him a home when he needed one. But he was mistaken, badly mistaken. We will keep an eye out for him, and try to help him if we can."

"You did well, agents. I'm taking you both out of the field for a nice, long break. And although we haven't the time or," he looked around the dark room, "resources for a formal ceremony, you're both promoted, effective immediately. Lizzie, I'd like you to commence with flight training. I think it's about time you knew how to land. And Hale..."

Jake nervously wondered what was in store for him.

"Agent Hale, I think it's time for you to go home."

"I could use the break," Jake said honestly.

The Colonel nodded briskly. "Very well. Get some food and a few hours of sleep, Hale, and we'll send you home in the morning."

Lizzie rose to leave the room, declaring herself equal parts starving and exhausted, but the Colonel coughed loudly. He held out his hand, open.

"Do I have to?" she asked.

He nodded seriously, and Lizzie plucked the knuckledusters from the depths of her pocket and dropped them into his waiting hand.

"I understand they were useful, but they were certainly not approved," the Colonel said. Lizzie looked remorseful for once.

"Sorry, sir. Hale, are you coming?"

Jake hesitated. "Could I talk to you for a minute, Colonel?"

The old man nodded, and Jake waited until the door was closed before speaking.

"I know this might sound strange, sir," Jake started, "but were you in Canada? I mean, at Vindiqo's offices? I saw someone on a security monitor, and it looked just like…" His words drifted off while Colonel Rex studied him, then sighed.

"No, Agent Hale, I was not in Canada, or anywhere near the Vindiqo labs."

"Then maybe Vindiqo has cameras in here! I promise you I saw—"

But Cyrus Rex put up his hand, and quieted Jake. "I know what you saw, Agent Hale, but these are things I can not discuss with you today, or tomorrow, or perhaps even next year. This is something I wish you hadn't seen, but you did. You are a conjurer, and you excel at confusion and misdirection. Remember, young man, that things are not always as they appear."

Jake nodded reluctantly, not understanding, and not entirely satisfied.

"And Agent Hale, when you get home, your parents…"

"Yeah?" Jake said.

The Colonel looked away. "Never mind. Just remember they love you very much."

"Ohhhkay," Jake said.

The Colonel cleared his throat and barked, "Agent dismissed!"

What was that all about? Jake wondered, but he was too tired to worry about it, so he just yawned and went to get some sleep.

Jenny, who'd been suffering from a stomach bug and was furious she'd missed such an eventful night, flew with Jake back to Oakland and drove him home from the airport.

The car stopped at the end of his driveway, and Jake looked out the window at his house for a long moment. The place looked smaller, somehow — but it also looked very welcome and inviting. His mom's cooking, his dad's bad jokes, his own bed... He couldn't wait to get back to all that. Being a secret agent was amazing, but it was nice to be home.

"Enjoy your break," Jenny said. "We'll be in touch to work out another visit to headquarters for proper training. Though you did amazingly well for someone who only had a day and a half with our instructors. You have good instincts."

"Not good enough. I never knew Filby was the traitor. I actually thought it was you."

Jenny pointed at herself with raised questioning eyebrows, and laughed. "Like I'd even have the time to be a double-agent."

Jake smiled, and slipped out of the car.

His dad met him at the door. "Welcome home, kid!" he said, bending down to give Jake a hug. "We missed you. Did you have fun at the lake?"

"Some," Jake said. "I helped save the world, but it turned out one of my friends was really a double agent working for the enemy."

"Well, nobody's perfect," his dad said. "Come on in. We'll order pizza."

Settling back into his normal old summer routine was strange. What did normal even mean anymore? Sleeping late, eating cereal for breakfast, watching cartoons, walking around the neighborhood — none of it seemed real anymore, somehow.

Jake read the news online, and found a story about the Vindiqo Research and Products Corporation closing down its Super Bee program because of "a technical hitch," which made him smile. The 49ers kickoff game went perfectly — and they won, too — although every article seemed to mention the curiously tight security at the stadium. And Jake also found a short story about a British beekeeper that lost his hives in a fire, and how local beekeepers donated enough bees for him to start up his hobby again. Jake wondered if he'd ever get to see the Beekeeper, and Mellifera Hall, again.

But there never was any news about Filby. What if Vindiqo had captured him? What if he was lost, alone, and scared in the wilds of Canada? Jake wasn't even able to talk to his parents about it. Late at night under the covers he'd start up his Stormpad and use his new security clearance to check, and to read through the Stormglass files now available to him, and learn more about the organization's past.

When his pals Aaron and Pete returned from camp, they boasted about their big adventures. Pete talked about how he'd swum with catfish, and caught one in his hands. His eyes flew up and to the right as he told the story. Aaron made them both promise to secrecy before he told them that he'd kissed Mimi from French class, and when Jake saw his eyes fly up and to the left, he smiled. One of them was lying. But Jake didn't care, he was just happy to have his two best friends back. He so desperately wanted to share his own stories — skydiving, secret bases, mad doctors and killer bees! — but he kept his mouth closed. His summer was a secret, and he didn't think his pals would believe him, anyway.

But they did pick up on some things.

"Why won't you eat VindiqoQo's anymore?" Aaron asked as he unwrapped an extra-large bar.

"Yeah, didn't you used to be a VindiqoQo fiend? And why are you learning Russian now?" laughed Pete. He snapped off a square of Aaron's candy bar, and popped it in his mouth. "Why would you spend your free time learning a language? It's not like you're going to Moscow anytime soon."

But Jake wasn't really listening. He was too busy eavesdropping on a suspiciously hushed conversation at the next table, and rolling a penny across his knuckles. As the last days of the summer drew to an end, he knew he'd changed inside.

Late one night, long after he'd finally fallen asleep, Jake's eyes shot open, though he wasn't sure why. There must have been a noise, but if so, he didn't hear it again. Jake pushed himself up on his elbows to look around his shadowy room, and had the weirdest feeling he wasn't alone.

"Hello?" he said, tentatively, but no one answered, of course.

Jake stared at the dark ceiling, holding his breath, and listening hard. What had awakened him?

He heard a soft sound of movement near his window, and whispered, "Lizzie?"

"Not quite," a voice said, and chuckled.

VIPERS AND SPIDERS

Jake rolled out of bed a moment before something heavy slammed against the mattress, but before he could get to his feet, someone kicked him in the side, knocking him against the bedframe, then stomped on his back, driving him belly-down on the floor. There were two people in his room, one on either side of his bed. The one who'd kicked him viciously wrenched his arm behind his back, pressing a knee against his spine at the same time.

"Don't scream," the boy whispered, "or we'll kill you. And then we'll kill your parents. Be good and you'll live. For now. Our granddaddy just wants us to hurt you a little. Break some fingers. Maybe turn your kneecaps around backwards. Show you what happens when you mess with the Chairman—"

There was a soft *phut phut* noise, and the boy pressing down on Jake's back groaned and fell over. Jake rolled to his side and scrambled back up onto the bed. There was someone crouched in his window, a figure visible only in silhouette. Jake flipped on the overhead light.

Filby was crouched in the window, pushing a pair of night vision goggles up on his forehead. He'd grown his hair long, and he held a tranquilizer gun in his hand. Jake stared at him, then looked at the twins, unconscious on the floor on either side of his bed.

"You... you're back!" Jake said.

"I was wondering, do you think I could come in from the cold?"

Jake broke into a grin as Filby climbed through the window, and gave him a big hug. Jake leaned over and picked up the weapon one of the twins had used to smack the bed.

"Hey, look — free hockey stick!"

THE END

THE STORMGLASS PROTOCOL

TIM PRATT AND ANDY DEEMER

ACKNOWLEDGEMENTS

Like many things, this book was born of secrecy, borders, and government lies.

I was running a propaganda magazine for the Chinese government in Beijing, when a strange envelope landed on my desk. "Highly Confidential," was stamped across the front, "To be opened only by the addressee." In the world of propaganda, this is surprisingly common. But what was inside the envelope was less common: a letter congratulating me on my large order from Gianelli's Bazaar of Fish. *I haven't ordered any fish,* I thought — confused — and meant to throw the letter away. I was interrupted by an apparently-urgent browbeating related to a statue of Chairman Mao and the word "Formosa" (a story for another day.)

Hours later I rediscovered the fishy letter still on my desk. *What is this*, I thought, finally giving in and visiting the website to collect my promised order of mackerel. Of course that site redirected me to Stormglass.com, the home of the secret (and very real) spy agency for children.

I was far too old to join Stormglass, I thought. But I wasn't too old to help tell their story with this book.

I would later discover that invitation was organized by my brother, creative-partner, and mentor Pete

Deemer — who'd become mixed up with the secret organization alongside his son Felix while living in India. My involvement, and the ensuing intrigue, danger and adventure, was entirely due to the two of them. The more they told me about Stormglass, the more ensnared I became. And so I gave notice at my government propaganda job, and set to work recording the story of Stormglass.

Felix and Pete, thank you. Your discovery of Stormglass changed my life. I'd like to think you both feel the same.

I'd of course like to thank Tim for creating such a grand story out of this secretive world, the amazing (yet never forgiving) editor David Kerrigan for his astute and insightful notes, and LeeAnn Deemer and Michelle Woo for their countless reads and wonderful feedback. Thanks also to Jenny Davidson for guiding us to Tim, Ginger Clark for developing that partnership, Ruth Kacher for her incredible feedback, and Tom Santosusso for his marketing wizardry. I do hate to name you here all, for fear of risking Vindiqo's fiery wrath, but so be it. Your guidance was without compare, my friends.

A special thank you to Stormglass Team Bangalore for bringing the agent tests to life at www.stormglass.com. Although I've encoded your names to protect your identities, you know who you are, Abhishek Agarwal, Anil Kumar, Ashish Gupta, Bijoy Thangaraj, Dharma Krish, Ebey Joseph, Khushboo Nagpal, Krishna S Raju, M Meidingoo Singh, Pradeep Bansal, Renuka, G Scott Taulbee,

Sindhoor Pangal, Uday Kumar, Varun Vasudev, and Yagnesh Ahir.

To Scott "Pop" McLean, the constant inventor, sometime poet, and original Cyrus Rex, and to his agents of PAJAM: before I'd heard of Stormglass, you were as close as it came to being real. And of course, thanks to Mom and Dad for mapping and paving our path to Stormglass, for making this all possible.

And finally, a special thank you to the next generation of Stormglass agents, most of all Nora and Loulou. Always watch the mailbox. You never know when a letter from Gianelli's Bazaar of Fish might arrive. If it does, open it. It could be for real.

- Andy Deemer, Bangalore, India

Thanks as always to my wife Heather and son River for giving me the time and space and support necessary to write; to my agent Ginger Clark for making the business side of my life run so smoothly; to Pete and Andy Deemer for giving me the security clearance to learn about Stormglass; to Ruth Katcher for her fantastic editing; and special thanks to Jenn Reese and Chris East for giving me the use of their guest room to hole up and write for a while — and to Chris again for allowing me access to the vast knowledge of spy films and literature that he keeps in his brain.

- Tim Pratt, Berkeley, California

ABOUT THE AUTHORS

Tim Pratt's fiction has won a Hugo Award, and has been a finalist for Sturgeon Memorial, Stoker, World Fantasy, Mythopoeic, and Nebula Awards, among others. His books include three short story collections, most recently *Antiquities and Tangibles and Other Stories*; a volume of poems; contemporary fantasy novels *The Strange Adventures of Rangergirl* and *Briarpatch*; science fantasy *The Nex*; steampunk novel *The Constantine Affliction* (as T. Aaron Payton); various roleplaying game tie-in fantasy novels; and, as T.A. Pratt, seven books (and counting) in an urban fantasy series about sorcerer Marla Mason. He works as a senior editor for Locus magazine, and lives in Berkeley CA with his wife Heather Shaw and their son River. Find him online at timpratt.org.

Andy Deemer is a writer, a fast-food horror filmmaker and a producer of videogames. Currently he lives in Bangalore with his girlfriend Michelle Woo and their bearded dog, Chop Suey. *The Stormglass Protocol* is his first novel.

Find out more about the world of Stormglass at

www.stormglass.com

Made in the USA
Lexington, KY
26 November 2013